I0573769

Romancing the Seas

Cait O'Sullivan

CRIMSON
ROMANCE
F+W Media, Inc.

Published by
Crimson Romance
an imprint of F+W Media, Inc.
10151 Carver Road, Suite 200
Blue Ash, Ohio 45242

www.crimsonromance.com

Copyright © 2012 by Cait O'Sullivan

ISBN 10: 1-4405-6261-X
ISBN 13: 978-1-4405-6261-7
eISBN 10: 1-4405-6262-8
eISBN 13: 978-1-4405-6262-4

Dedication

For my family, a constant source of optimism and encouragement.
Neecy, Steph and the wonderful Jennifer at Crimson, Jonathon and Pippa wouldn't have made it off the page without you.
Big thanks.

Chapter One

Pippa Renshaw took a deep breath and reached for the door. The well-oiled hinges swung open too easily and she nearly fell into the hotel reception area from the stair well. An anxious giggle started in the pit of her tummy and her hand flew to her forehead to hide her face, even as she steadied herself on the jamb to look around.

If she had been in any other situation than that of meeting her new boss, she would have laughed aloud with nerves as everyone in the foyer stared. It reminded her of going into a little country pub, where newcomers intrigued the regulars. Was it like that everywhere in New Zealand? And where was her new boss? Looking around, she couldn't see him anywhere.

Her gaze flickered over two suited executives and away, but as though elastic, it was pulled straight back again. Her tummy felt like it was careering down the stairs as liquid gold eyes pierced hers, arousing feelings of familiarity. But she'd surely remember a man so attractive if she had met him before.

Pippa shook her head slightly to shift the cloud of confusion clamping down over her tired brain, shocked by the heat his gaze ignited deep within her. Embarrassed at her reaction, she lowered her eyes, sure her attraction to him flickered within them for all to see. Yet she couldn't prevent her gaze from lingering over a set of broad shoulders, encased in a white shirt, sleeves rolled up to show strong forearms resting on long, muscular thighs.

Yummy!

Her gaze roamed further all of its own accord, enjoying the sharp square edges to his jaw, lightly flecked with stubble, the cleft in his chin, the full lower lip, the Roman nose, and those impossibly golden eyes. Eyes that were watching her with an amused expression.

Electric mortification shot through her.

The shock brought control back to her. Momentarily. She winced whilst raising a shaky hand to try to smooth down her curls.

A fine time to be looking such a mess.

His companion tapped at a sheet in front of them, and like a liquid golden sunray dissipating, the man's gaze left her.

Feeling cold, Pippa hauled her attention back to the here and now.

Where was she again? Oh yeah. Auckland, meeting her new boss. Shame he was a not-so-attractive middle-aged man and not a drop dead gorgeous specimen like Hotty over there. Actually scratch that, who wanted sexual attraction at work? Certainly not her, not anymore.

*

Jonathon Eagleton gazed unseeingly at the accounts in front of him. A breath of fresh air had blown through the staid five-star Stevenson Hotel when the fire door had opened to frame an image, a vision, a what?

Whatever or whoever she was, she stole his breath. Auburn hair tumbled around her shoulders, and her cheeks flushed despite a heaving chest trying to keep oxygen in good supply. He had seen a mischievous twinkle in her eyes as she'd glanced around, only for her gaze to hook on his.

Yes, he had been staring—what man wouldn't, after all? Her simple green t-shirt hugged firm breasts, tapering to a slim waist and faded denims encasing long legs. He'd watched with increasing interest as she made a leisurely inspection of him. Visions of her hands following her gaze had caused his skin to tighten, and when her green eyes lit on his, a spark had shot through him, inciting blatant desire.

He almost got up there and then to…what? Drag her off to his cave? Crazy thoughts.

He turned back to his laptop, shaking his head to rid himself of her, and his temples throbbed with renewed vigour. As the newly hired CEO of Queen Cruises, he was fire fighting, hurtling headlong from one disaster to another. He had enough on his plate as it was.

He drummed his fingers on the table, stifling a sigh. It was only his second day on the job. His first day had gone down in history as utterly shambolic, and it looked as though today was going the same way. This meeting over-ran as he kept discovering things that warranted his immediate attention, and his next meeting hadn't even showed.

But he hadn't risen to the role of CEO by the age of thirty-seven for nothing. He hadn't failed yet, and didn't intend this stint at Queen Cruises to besmirch his excellent reputation.

He looked at his accountant, watching the redhead walk through the lobby out of the corner of his eye. "Queen Cruises are missing seven million dollars, Steve." He gestured at the figures on his laptop screen. "These accounts could win a cooking competition."

Steve shook his head, pulling a crooked smile. "Mulberry was a pro at conning the company. I would say he pocketed the profit for his entire three years as CEO."

Jonathon placed his elbows on his knees and raked his hands through his hair.

"But what about James Houghton? Did he not notice anything?" It was unthinkable that the chief financial officer wouldn't have been holding a tight rein on the company's money.

"They were all in on it. I only joined six months ago, but the corruption was obvious. However, now that you're on board—if you'll excuse the pun—that's going to change."

Jonathon leaned back into his chair, putting one arm over the back. He smiled. "Damn right it is. The first major change is to make you CFO. I need to know I have a man I can trust in charge of finances."

Steve stared at him with a shocked expression. "I have no experience as CFO."

"Well, you soon will. Congratulations." Jonathon put out his hand and shook Steve's. "But it's not going to be easy—your first task is to claw back that seven million."

And to find out who the redhead is... Shame the role of CFO didn't encompass investigating for the CEO.

Jonathon tapped his finger against his cheek. "What about the customer accommodation expansion, how did it go? I see we overspent on our budget."

"Very well, actually," replied Steve. "With one exception. When they ran out of space, Mulberry gave them the all clear to expand into the staff quarters—so now we are one down on staff accommodation. But he probably didn't worry about that, if you catch my drift." Steve shifted in his chair.

"Care to expand?" Jonathon looked at Steve and narrowed his eyes, knowing what he was going to hear.

"It just meant someone would share his bed when he was on board. When he interviewed, the good-looking girls invariably got the job, and if they had any friends looking for a job, then they got one too. Mulberry wasn't too picky about their capabilities as long as they were sufficiently, how shall I put it, *grateful* to him." Steve nodded at him, a weary expression in his eyes. "I think that's what happened with your new head chef of Corals restaurant, as I know Elizabeth Rankin, the previous sous-chef—not greatly talented—who enjoyed an easy ride in the kitchen recommended her."

Lips tightly compressed, Jonathon shook his head and added *head chef of Corals Restaurant* to the list of employees for checking out.

The sound of an English accent broke through to him and he heard the redhead ask at the reception desk for Mulberry.

"Case in point." Steve pulled a wry smile in the general direction of reception. "It's not as if she isn't good-looking, is it? And now, if you'll excuse me, I have to go and check on orders for tomorrow."

"Fine, fine," said Jonathon, concentrating instead on the girl's voice. So *she* was Mulberry's latest acquisition. Damned shame. Just when he thought she looked interesting. He prayed the sous-chef would be worth his salt.

Standing up, he strode over to the redhead. He looked pointedly at his Breitling watch and thrust his hand toward her. "Jonathon Eagleton." He bit his name out. "You're late."

*

It was him! Oh my God!

Pippa could have cried. It had been a long couple of days, and here was a man who reduced her to a quivering wreck. Her thoughts were all a jumble—what she wouldn't give to be back in England with no devastatingly attractive man clearly annoyed by her very presence right in front of her.

"It's a pleasure to meet you, Mr. Eagleton," she said with a smile that, try as she might, she couldn't quite force into her eyes. "Had I known it was Mr. Eagleton and not Mr. Mulberry meeting me, I would have left a message for you, rather than him. I had a ten-hour delay in Melbourne, so I just got in the door. I haven't even had time to change. However, I called the hotel from the stopover and asked them to pass the message on."

"Well, you should have left it for Queen's Cruises, rather than a named associate. Anything could have happened, and as it turned out, anything did." His English accent gave his words an added edge and she flinched inside with each crisp articulation. He towered over her, implacable, a hard edge to his jaw.

Adrenaline pulled her back from the brink of tears. "Well, I do apologise. I didn't know. I got here as soon as I could and haven't had time to freshen up since my flight. I even ran down twelve flights of stairs because the lift isn't working." It was rare she felt like a naughty child, and the feeling wasn't a very comfortable one.

She satisfied herself by returning his bad-tempered look, putting the full force of her jetlag and exasperation with discourteous men into her gaze. A picture could tell a thousand words and she was sure she was a portrait of annoyance.

"Mulberry has left the company." His words were glacial.

"Right, so who is in charge then?"

"I am. I'm the new CEO."

Pippa stared in disbelief. The feelings this man inspired in her were nothing short of cataclysmic. She felt like she was finishing a marathon, head spinning and running on instinct. Which told her this man was dangerous. The similarities—arrogance and impatience—between him and Marcus were already there. And look what Marcus had done to her.

She shivered suddenly with a premonition. Jonathon Eagleton was overpowering, and she would be helpless if ever he turned his charm on her. She swayed on her feet, and just stopped herself from clutching at his arm.

He put out his hand to steady her and looked irritated at the touch, which seared through her skin to imprint itself on her very bones. "I appreciate this is a surprise to you. Mulberry left very suddenly." He eyed her and giving a half nod, gestured over to his table. "I have another hour's work to do here. Why don't you go and freshen up, and see me back down here when you're ready."

"Okay, thanks." Pippa felt she should have said something else, but she was just too darned overwhelmed and not very capable anymore. Turning on her heel, she walked over to the fire exit door.

"Ms. Renshaw?"

What did he want now? She glanced around to see him pointing to the lobby.

"The lifts seem to be working."

"Okay, thanks." Hadn't she already said that? Great, he had her reduced to a parrot, and not a very intelligent one, either. When the lift pinged its arrival, she fled into the corner to be out of his line of sight.

She reached her light, airy room in a daze and walked through it, shedding her clothes, wishing she could shed her thoughts as easily. Unease shifted around her lower tummy, bringing with it a feeling of foreboding. Probably just the jetlag combined with the lack of sleep and food. Nothing whatsoever to do with that man downstairs.

She turned on the shower jets and tried to scrub away the image of him looking up at her as she had walked through the door, but it was no good. Whenever she closed her eyes, she could see his dark eyes piercing her soul. Her blood shivered as she remembered the unfathomable look in his eyes. Her earlier impression of golden eyes was wrong, they were tawny but with come hither flecks of gold. A girl could lose herself in such a look. Would he save her if she did? She groaned aloud, resting her head against the tiled wall.

They were destined to have a working relationship. But no more. On the bright side, at least they weren't going to be shoulder to shoulder as she had been with Marcus. She'd be damned if she would let herself go down the same route again. Sleeping with the boss, no matter how many times he declared undying love, was a mistake made only once.

Never again.

She needed to stay away from Jonathon. He was the CEO after all, the man in charge of the company, and would have little to do with her. She took out her only set of good clothes—slim leg black trousers with a cream silk blouse—and armed herself with pep talk as she dressed.

Last meeting with him for a while so let's get it over with and then stay as far away as possible.

She grabbed her bag and walked out the door, head held high. She could do this.

As she stepped out of the lift, her gaze flew impatiently to his. Yup, darn it, the same sizzling attraction simmered. He was on his mobile, ankle of one leg atop knee of the other, and his arm stretched along the back of the chair. He nodded to her and gestured at the chairs in front of him, carrying on talking.

Pippa folded herself into the chair, crossing her ankles neatly and casting her gaze around for something to look at, rather than him.

Hurry up, I want this over with.

He wrapped up the call, dropping the phone on the low coffee table in front of them.

"I've ordered some sandwiches and a pot of tea." He gave her a half smile. "You do drink tea, I assume, being English?"

Pippa smiled to herself, briefly flirting with the thought of saying no to what sounded like an accusation, but the desire for a nice cup of tea won out. "I do. Lovely, thanks."

"Good." He looked at her as if seeing her properly for the first time. Pippa's toes curled, and she distracted herself by trying to read his illegible notes on the table. Did he have any idea what he was doing to her?

Jonathon leafed through his papers until he came to the one he wanted, and holding it up, frowned at her. "Mr. Mulberry has left no interview details and no notes except when and where he was due to meet you. All I have are your references. Do you have a copy of your CV?"

Pippa handed over her manila folder, thanking her lucky stars she had thought to bring it. "I attended Catering College in England and came top of my class with a First. One of my friends there, a girl called Elizabeth Rankin, worked for Mr. Mulberry and suggested I get in touch about the position of head chef. She said she would recommend me, and Mr. Mulberry seemed delighted he didn't have to advertise."

He took her CV, throwing it on the table without even glancing at it. Pippa could've sworn his lip curled as he did so. "So where did you interview?"

"He was in London, passing through, and I met him there."

"I see." Jonathon drew the word out, and Pippa understood how a mouse might feel faced with a fierce cat closing in on it. There was a pause, and she struggled not to fidget and to meet his direct gaze. What was his problem?

He broke the awkwardness. "Tell me about your previous position."

"I worked as sous chef for Marcus Longbottom for four years, and have worked in each of his double Michelin starred-restaurants around London." As Pippa spoke, she drew herself up in her chair, and her voice lost its shake. It had been hard work, but she had risen to the challenge and had made quite a name for herself as an up and coming young chef.

"He's got a first-class reputation; you must be good at what you do." Jonathon's tawny eyes sharpened on her face as he said this.

To her chagrin, her cheeks heated and she looked at her shoes. A few people she worked with had been jealous of her success. As a result, rumours were rife, saying she had risen to the top so quickly by sleeping with the boss. She felt, rather than saw, the keen look Jonathon gave her. She was being put through the wringer here.

"Why did you leave?" he asked.

"It was time to move on." Pippa ignored her flush and raised her chin determinedly. She was a good chef, whether this guy believed it or not.

"To a ship cruising New Zealand? Hardly the place for a young rising star such as yourself."

The caustic note in his voice set Pippa's teeth on edge, but she gritted them and kept quiet. He looked at her for a long moment, then shot a wrist out to look at his watch and frowned.

"Down to business. Jean-Pierre, the current head chef, is not available. Also, I have some bad news, I'm afraid."

Pippa's eyes flew to his. He was going to tell her she no longer had a job. She should have known better than to trust Mulberry, who told her not to worry about details and he would sort it all out. She frowned. Her flight had cleared out her meagre savings; she didn't even have the money to get home.

"You are the last employee hired. We are a bed short, so you have no staff accommodation." Pippa felt a small measure of relief—at least she had a job with a salary. She would sleep in a lifeboat for all it mattered to her.

"I will be on board, doing some corporate entertaining and residing in the company suite. When I say suite, it has two bedrooms, a large double and a smaller version. Both fortunately en-suite. There is a dining room, a sitting room with a sleeper couch, a bathroom, and a small kitchen. So if you want this job…" He stopped and looked questioningly at her. Throat suddenly dry, she nodded reluctantly. "You have no choice but to share with me. Oh good, here are the sandwiches."

Oh dear God, I don't believe it.

Wave after wave of horror washed over her as she realised what the next couple of weeks were going to mean to her. A new, stressful job and sharing a suite with her obnoxious—if highly attractive—boss. Her image of a new life was starting to crumble around her before she had a chance to place even one brick there herself.

"Share with you? Is there nowhere else I can stay?" She held her hands out imploringly.

"Obviously, Ms. Renshaw, I wouldn't give up my privacy unless it was absolutely required. Don't worry, at least you'll have your own bed." He cocked an eyebrow as he raised his tea to his lips, a knowing look in his eyes.

Shock slammed into her. Had he heard about her and Marcus? Despite the rumours, they had been extremely discreet, and only a handful of other people knew the truth about them. Had

Elizabeth known? Pippa doubted, but even if she had, Elizabeth had left after recommending her.

She narrowed her eyes, her good intentions of keeping calm unravelling. "Mr. Eagleton, if I had the money, I assure you, I'd be on the next flight out of here. I don't like the idea of sharing anything with you anymore than you do. But you need a head chef, and I need a job. That's the bottom line. And now, if you'll excuse me, I need to get some fresh air." Her voice wobbled on the last word. She had to get away from him—tears weren't far away. Drat this impossible man.

Pippa rose from the sofa, part of her registering him standing as she stood. Hah, a bit late to show some manners. She headed out through the main entrance and turned sharply to the right as though she knew where she was going. Following the path, she ended up at the marina and stood in front of all the pretty yachts, breathing deeply.

The wind blew gently through the harbour, causing the rigging of the boats to rattle against the masts in an eerie clanking noise. *Go home, go home*, they whispered. Pippa sank onto a bench and watched the yachts.

Could she cope with sharing a cabin with him? No, far better she phoned her mum and asked her to transfer enough funds to see her home. *And what?* a small voice asked. *Go back to Marcus? Find a job in London and see Marcus all over the gossip magazines with his latest girlfriend?*

Given the choices, staying would be the least painful.

Chapter Two

Jonathon took a bite from his sandwich. She must be a good liar. Her face had been guileless, honest, and open—one, present circumstances removed, Jonathon liked.

However, the facts were stark. Mulberry was a well-known sleaze, and Pippa's friend must have made her aware of that fact. Had she already slept with him or was she planning on doing so? Maybe it was a condition of hire. Jonathon certainly hadn't had the opportunity to ask when he'd had the bad fortune to bump into him.

A cold snap went through him at the thought of his only meeting with Mulberry. With the thought of customer entertainment on his mind, he had gone out to the Coral Princess, docked in the bay, to check out his suite, The Doubtful. He thought he had heard something as he put the key in the lock. He had been right. Mulberry, *in flagrante* with a woman who transpired to be a new housekeeper, showed no shame. All very galling.

Jonathon shook himself mentally and tried to avoid the image of Pippa in the housekeeper's place. She certainly knew how to stand up for herself, but guilt shone from her expressive face. She was hiding something. He sighed. Typical. He'd met a woman who could turn out to be intriguing—not that he would find out—and she was a woman without scruples. Not the kind of woman Jonathon liked.

On the plus side, her references were excellent; in fact, looking at the one from Marcus Longbottom, he hadn't ever read such a glowing recommendation. And a First from the Winchester Hotel and Catering College, a world-renowned catering school. He knew a professor there; he must drop him an email and see what he made of Pippa Renshaw.

Of course, Pippa still had the job—there was no time to re-interview and find someone else capable of running Corals Restaurant before they set sail.

He called a waiter over and quickly scribbled a note. "Deliver this to Ms. Renshaw's room please, along with the tea and sandwiches." He shut his laptop lid with a click and stood to go to his next meeting with the Stevenson family. They were world-renowned hoteliers, a three thousand strong chain of five star hotels to their name, and looking into the possibility of branching out with a cruise partner. They wanted to be able to promise the same Stevenson luxury whether travelling abroad or over the seas.

Since they were joining the cruise, Jonathon had no choice but to go along as well to do some serious schmoozing. He could ill afford the time, there being so much to sort out at board level, but then again, the deal on the table would considerably help the ailing finances of Queen Cruises should he close it. The Stevensons were in talks with several cruise companies—not just his—and Jonathon wanted to nail this deal.

*

Pippa panicked when she heard the knock on her door. Her eyes were red, her face blotchy, and her senses quailed at the thought of further onslaught. When she looked through the spy hole, sweet relief swam through her when nothing scarier than a waiter stood there, holding a tray on which sandwiches were laid out alongside a fresh pot of tea. But a note nestled in between the salt and pepper rang alarm bells.

Oh God, was he firing her for being so belligerent? Who could blame him? Now that her emotions were a bit calmer, she could see her reaction had not been in the interest of diplomatic job relations. Plus, not having her on board would save him having to share his suite. She slowly opened the door, as though to delay the inevitable, and accepted the tray, muttering her thanks through tight lips.

Tea wasn't what she needed anymore—a shot of brandy would do the trick much better. She scanned the note with one eye scrunched up, then both flew open in shock. She still had the job. But the ship departed Auckland tomorrow at ten a.m.

Surely there was some mistake. She had been under the impression that the Princess Coral left a week from tomorrow. Mr. Mulberry certainly wasn't too hot on details. A new nervous knot joined the one already in her stomach. Mr. Eagleton expected her to report to the ship at six a.m.

She sat with a thump on the bed. Could her day get any worse? Sharing a suite with him as of *tomorrow*? How would she cope? She knew nothing about her new kitchen, since she'd assumed she had a week to get to know the ins and outs before they set sail.

Heedless of how she looked, she raced downstairs. Two other people now sat at the coffee table. She strode into the bar—no sign of him there either. Going back to reception, she rang the bell impatiently.

"Yes, madam?" The same receptionist who had witnessed Pippa's first meeting with her new CEO looked at her, sympathy in her brown eyes.

"I'm looking for Mr. Eagleton, do you know where he is?" Pippa drummed her fingers on the highly polished top.

"I think he's in one of the conference rooms, in a meeting."

Pippa stared at the receptionist and shook her head slightly, rolling her eyes.

"Well, if he gets out soon, will you please give him this?" She wrote a note asking him to call her room, trying not to break the pen as she did so, and caught the lift back up to her room to wait.

Yet she couldn't sit still. Her mind raced, unanswered questions feeding the frenzied flock of butterflies in her stomach. The hotel brochure caught her attention and she flicked through it until she came to the leisure facilities. Great, she needed a good run. Either that or pace the small room until the carpet wore down.

She changed quickly and jumped two-at-a-time down the hotel stairs to the gym in the basement. There were several top-of-the-range treadmills and she chose one, slowly working her stride. But her mind refused to let up. Why had she come out here to New Zealand? She should have stayed in London, working for Marcus. Okay, maybe she would have moved to a different restaurant, but even then she would have been surrounded by the familiar, not the unknown—and the downright scary. Now she was a prisoner of her own design: new country—heck, new *continent*—new job, new boss, no friends, and not even any space to call her own.

Pippa heaved a sigh, then took lots of little breaths to make up for her hard working lungs. Oh, who knows, maybe she had done the right thing. How could she have stayed in London after what Marcus had done? An up and coming celebrity chef, she had supported him all the way. Until his publicist had said to him, "Lose the sous chef; she's too ordinary a look for you. You need an *it* girl on your arm, so all the paparazzi will be snapping you for the celebrity magazines."

"Look, Pippa," Marcus had pleaded. "Just give me a couple of years to get to the top of my career and then we can be together properly. We can still be together, but just keep our relationship under cover."

Pippa had wanted to cry, but instead picked up her bag and walked out of the flat she had never quite moved into.

She *had* been right to leave. But whether she had been right to leave so drastically, swapping everything she had ever known for the unknown, was very questionable.

Her heart pounded rapidly and she pressed the treadmill button to lower the speed, concentrating on breathing deeply to slow her heart rate down. A light cough from the treadmill beside her nearly threw her off her treadmill in surprise.

Her new roomie.

In an attempt not to let the machine sweep her off, she pumped her legs and finally caught back up with the pace. Great. Glances at the monitor, proudly proclaiming a heart rate of 190, made her want to curl up and die. Mr. Eagleton, on the other hand, appeared very relaxed and loose limbed beside her as he lengthened into his pace, despite a faint sheen of sweat—clearly he had been in the gym for a while.

Breathe.

"Are you okay?" He didn't look at her as he asked, he just kept running.

Okay? Sure, if you call just having learnt I have to share a suite with you, starting from tomorrow, okay.

She breathed deeply, trying to use mind over body to slow her heart. God forbid, he may look over, see the state of her, and think it was his effect on her. Or she was desperately unfit. Which would her pride prefer?

"Fine. You?" Being economical with her words was a necessity.

"Yup."

Pippa's head felt bogged down in quicksand and her heart stubbornly refused to go below 190.

"Did you get my note?" His tone was curt.

She nodded and then, feeling she let herself down, hit the speed to bring the treadmill down to a fast walking pace. Having a conversation whilst running proved impossible.

"I did, yeah. Did you get mine?" Picking up her bottle of water, she took a big glug, welcoming the coolness.

"No." She could feel him looking at her through the mirrors in front of them.

"I thought we weren't leaving until this day next week." She met his gaze. Her tummy decided to get in on the fitness malarkey and started doing somersaults. He looked very fit with an easy lope to his running Pippa envied, carrying his six foot plus frame easily.

"Well, sorry." There was no shortage of breath despite running at—quick glance at his monitor—10k an hour.

"I have so many questions. I thought we were berthed for another week, plenty of time for me to get to know the ship and Coral's kitchen." She could hear her voice becoming thinner, and stopped.

He glanced sideways at her, a slight smile on his face, making it quite clear he was enjoying his game of cat and mouse. "I assumed you knew the departure date of the Coral Princess."

Pippa walked at a slow pace now, breathing deeply, up through her diaphragm and out through her nose, but it didn't help. Her heart rate remained at 150.

"Well, you said so yourself, Mr. Mulberry made a lot of mistakes. One of them was telling me the wrong departure date. I don't know anything about Coral's kitchen, and so I'd appreciate hearing everything you can tell me about it."

Jonathon's answer to her was to increase his speed. "You'll find out all you need to know tomorrow. In the meantime I suggest you catch up on some sleep and I'll see you on board in the morning."

Blast the man. He wasn't going to give her any respite from worrying.

One last try.

"Perhaps then we could share a taxi to the port so you can enlighten me on the way?"

Jonathon flicked out his iPod headphones from the carrier on his wrist and started unwinding them, loping beside her. "I don't think that's a very good idea, do you? People may get the wrong impression."

He fixed the headphones into his ears, nodded to her, and increased his pace yet again.

Conversation clearly closed.

Pippa hit the red stop button, not caring about cooling down. Towelling her neck and forehead, she stalked—as much as her tired legs would allow her—into the changing room to swap her gym gear for her swimsuit. The man was so annoying. How would she share his suite without giving him a piece of her mind?

The pool had looked inviting when she glanced in before her run. Small, but spot lit from below the water level, which cast a lovely warm glow throughout the turquoise water. The lights around the pool were placed strategically behind the palm plants and piano music played over the tannoy. Nobody else swimming.

In other words, heaven.

She dived into the deep end and emerged half way down the pool. This was far better than cooling down on the treadmill beside that insufferable man. Pippa luxuriated in the long stretches her body took through the water, her aching legs having a new lease on life. She powered through the water, not pausing to stop until half an hour had passed on the clock. Feeling she then deserved it, she took a break—she rested her head on her arms folded on the side of the pool, and let her legs kick out behind her.

The door opened to admit Jonathon, towel thrown over one shoulder. Typical. She couldn't go anywhere now without seeing him. The sensation of seeing him slammed into her tummy.

Unable to resist, she peered over the side of the pool to watch him hang his towel up by hers and take a quick shower, pushing his hair back out of his eyes with both hands. He looked darn hot, swimming shorts showing off his long muscular thighs and washboard stomach, biceps bunching as he rubbed at his hair. Those arms around her would make her feel feminine and petite—not an easy task, as she stood five foot nine and gym fit and slender rather than skinny. He looked strong enough to pick her up and chuck her over his shoulder, and the thought had her poor overworked heart racing again. Where were her thoughts taking her? This was her new boss, her new *roommate*, for Pete's sake. Time to get a grip.

Jonathon turned off the shower and advanced toward the pool, and Pippa shrank by the edge, ducked her head underwater to cool down, and blew out air to make bubbles. His feet appeared within an inch of where she clutched on for dear life, and he dived in.

No time to be lost. Pippa hauled herself out of the pool, ran for her towel, and headed back through to the changing room. As she went through the swing door, she chanced a look back at the pool, only to see him at the other end, watching her. Her body flushed nearly hot enough to dry her swimsuit. Hopefully he wasn't going to appear in the changing room too.

*

Jonathon lapped up and down the pool, deploring the fact that six strokes covered the length of it. He seemed to be constantly tumble turning, to emerge halfway down the pool, a few strokes, and tumble turning again. It was difficult to maintain any kind of rhythm. Giving up, he went to the shower, trying to pull his mind back from seeing Pippa do the same.

She obviously worked out; her impressive run showcased her fitness. He'd spotted her as soon as he came into the gym, and had kept an eye on her whilst warming up and doing some weights.

Then when she scrambled out of the pool, her pert bum in a cut away costume, his throat went dry at the thought of caressing it. Her legs were long and toned, with slim calves tapering away into very sexy ankles. His imagination turned the page, and he saw her in a green satin dress clinging to her curves and killer heels, looking teasingly over her shoulder at him. Masses of curls piled high on her head, with a few escaping, and lips pouting in a very kissable expression. Pippa on his arm at the end-of-year company ball would ensure no end of jealous looks his way.

This was ridiculous. He was the CEO, she the newly hired head-chef, and he had to keep his reputation intact. Especially coming after Mulberry. Pippa wasn't a siren bestowed with the power to entrance him. He must think of the Stevensons. His muscles unclenched, and he allowed his mind to take him down the much-travelled path to work.

*

As Pippa sat in the lobby the next morning waiting for the doorman to get her a taxi, she found herself disagreeing with whoever penned the phrase "everything looks better in the morning." Little things (was her case too big for the suite?) up to the big things (how on earth would she manage?) competed in her mind as to which could knot her gut the most.

Catching sight of Jonathon standing at the door glued to his phone, Pippa realised it was a no-brainer—he caused the ultimate twist.

Get a grip. He's only a man. Relax. And you, heart, just do your normal everyday business. Don't go speeding up on me. Chill.

A girl checking out caught her eye and waved. Hurrying over, she collapsed on the sofa next to her. "Hi, I'm Fiona. Mr. Eagleton asked me yesterday to look out for you and to stick by you until you find your sea legs. I came in late last night; otherwise, I would have rung and introduced myself. I'm the front office manager, in charge of customer accommodation." The Irish lilt to Fiona's words, as well as the words themselves, put Pippa instantly at ease with the older girl.

"I'm Pippa. It's lovely to meet you."

But Fiona's gaze was focused over Pippa's shoulder. "He's gorgeous, isn't he?" Fiona indicated Jonathon's departing back. "All the girls are mad about him and some of the men too," she said with raised eyebrows and a giggle.

"I'm sure," murmured Pippa, not really wanting to get into this conversation.

"How are you? Are you looking forward to your first couple of weeks on board?"

"I am, yes, thanks."

"Jean-Pierre is around for another week—he's a complete sweetheart. There will be plenty of time for you to get to know everybody, and the ins and outs of the kitchen. Come on, here's a taxi for us." Fiona stood up and waited for Pippa to go out ahead of her to the waiting taxi.

With a palpable sigh, Pippa sank back into the back seat. Thankfully, she wasn't going to be on her own in a new kitchen. Her gut-wrenching nerves calmed and fizzy excitement filled her blood to race around her body. She stared out the window, eager for her first glimpse of her new home. When she did see the ship, she took her breath away.

Majestic in the water and definitely the queen of the bay, the Princess Coral dwarfed all other floating vessels, rendering them her faithful servants, there to pay homage. Pride glimmered Pippa's heart; it would be no mean feat to be associated with this beauty. There was the ubiquitous swimming pool, a small ice rink, a climbing wall, a spa, and a gym. Everything needed to pamper the passengers. A small floating city, she had five different catering establishments ranging from coffee and snacks up to the elegant five-star restaurant, Corals, catering for every taste bud.

Unable to stay away for even a minute longer, Pippa headed to the kitchen to ask for Jean-Pierre. The glance she got from him told her he wasn't expecting anything great from her. Quite the opposite, in fact. She inwardly sighed; being Mr. Mulberry's latest recruit wasn't doing her any favours.

The kitchen was compact, sure, but well equipped with gleaming work surfaces. Her pride took on a new shine—this would be her domain soon. The thought gave her the energy to keep up with Jean-Pierre as he spoke rapidly and strode through the kitchen. This was going to be exhausting. Yet he stopped when she mentioned Marcus Longbottom.

"'e was a good man to work for, you are a lucky lady. I trained with 'im some time ago. You must be a very good chef." His eyes sharpened on her face as he spoke, and he gave her a half smile. From then on, Pippa peppered him with excited questions and he answered them all with great deliberation. By the end of a couple of hours shadowing him, Pippa had a lot of confidence in both the kitchen and the staff. Excitement seamlessly mixed with nerves. If only she had some other accommodation, she would be enjoying herself. Yet every time she thought of the suite, her heart plummeted as though someone had just thrown it over the side of the ship.

"And then of course, you 'ave the Captain's Dinner." They were in the small office to the side of the kitchen as Jean-Pierre talked through the culinary activity of the next two weeks. Pippa had half an eye on the kitchen out through the window, liking the fact she would work in here and still see what went on. "The cruise ends there for you. The evening is very special: we 'ave a five-course menu, each course served with a complementing wine, and the night is generally regarded as the Grand Ball of the voyage. I am sure with your abilities you will 'ave no problem, no problem at all."

Pippa nodded, but to her a five-course meal for two hundred people sounded like it would present a few challenges.

Fiona passed by the window, and stopped when she saw them. She popped her head around the ajar door. "I'm heading to the staff canteen, do you want to come?"

Pippa nodded, then turned to thank Jean-Pierre.

When they reached the deck, Pippa looked out at the view, and a smile sprang to her lips as she took in the Hauraki Gulf passing before them on their way to Mercury Island.

"I can't wait to get out hiking when we dock at Milford Sound," she said.

"We get a break before then. We stop at Kaikoura for the passengers to disembark until the following morning, so we're all free for twenty-four hours. Mind you, I don't know who you'll get to go hiking, we're not a very active bunch here." Fiona gave a half-smile.

"Oh, I don't mind, I like hiking on my own."

As they entered the small canteen, a babble of noise greeted them, and Fiona stood on her tiptoes to look around and waved to someone she spotted. "Come and meet my boyfriend, David. He's the head chef for the Chinese restaurant, and the steakhouse."

David stood as the girls arrived. "Hello, Pippa, I'm pleased to meet you. Do let me know if there's anything I can do to help you settle in." He slipped an arm around Fiona's waist. "Hey, sweetheart, have you heard who's on board yet?"

"No?" Fiona glanced at Pippa, eyebrows raised.

"Well..." said David, teasingly drawing it out. "You'll know the daughter from all the celebrity magazines you buy. Our new, esteemed CEO is wining and dining her family."

"Who is it?" demanded Fiona.

"It's the Stevensons, from Stevenson Hotels!"

Fiona shrieked. "I don't believe it, no way, not on board here! How cool! Is Juliet here?"

Juliet Stevenson, the heiress, was always gracing the magazines with her nonchalant style and not-so-nonchalant escapades.

David nodded.

"Wow," breathed Fiona, yet to return to earth. "I can't wait to see her. I wonder what she'll be wearing."

So that was who Jonathon was going to be entertaining. Good luck to him. Juliet was, if the magazines were anything to go by, notoriously high maintenance. Oh God. What if he had plans to entertain her in the suite they were sharing? She could just imagine coming in after her shift, greeted by low lights, sultry music, and him moving in for a kiss. Could this get any worse?

"Onto even more exciting things." David leaned across the table with a gleam in his eyes. "I hear you've got some great accommodation, Pippa!"

Pippa opened her mouth to answer when she heard a commotion at the door. One of the commis chefs she'd met earlier in Corals kitchen came in, calling for her.

"I'm here," she called, nerves starting anew.

"Hi," he called, and made his way over, stopping to say hi to a few people on the way as Pippa's heart skipped several beats. "I've a message for you from Mr. Eagleton. He's having the Stevensons to dinner in the executive dining room and wants you to cook."

Pippa stared at him. "What, tonight?"

"He wants to meet you in the kitchen now."

Chapter Three

Pippa left the staff canteen and the sound of laughter behind as she headed to see Jonathon. By the time she reached the kitchen, nausea swirled seamlessly with her tiredness. He stood by the office door in the near empty kitchen, looking through some papers.

"Pippa, glad to see you got the message. Come over, please."

"Yes, Mr. Eagleton, what can I do for you?"

"Jean-Pierre is busy with the opening ball tonight, so I need you to cook for me and the Stevensons. We are out to impress, so please ensure it is cooked well. Also, I should be the one to show you to your home for the next two weeks. On the way, we can discuss the menu." He moved toward the door and Pippa stepped into pace, thanking her lucky stars she knew exactly what the kitchen carried.

"I think we should keep it simple. A hot starter, then a chicken main course followed by a nice dessert and cheese. I'll leave the details up to you. I do know the Stevensons have no dietary restrictions, so prepare whatever you think will wow them." Jonathon looked at her, but Pippa kept her gaze pinned to the floor.

"Yes, sure, what time would you like to eat?" Amazed her words came out clearly, Pippa tried to ignore the thumping of her heart. They were on the way to see their suite. She, who couldn't even share with her sister now had to share with an unfamiliar and, yeah, let's face it, drop-dead gorgeous bloke. Not to forget he was her boss too. Oh God, they were slowing down…

"About nine, please. Here it is." He opened a door and stood back.

Pippa swallowed to get rid of the lump in her throat and went in ahead of Jonathon, straight into the living room, decked out

29

in coffee and cream colours. A large sofa drew the eye straight to it. Despite the early hour, the lamps threw a clear glow onto the countryside paintings scattered throughout. Light gauze curtains of the palest blue swept inwards from a breeze off the balcony. A small oak bar curved into a corner, opposite of which the television—all fifty-two inches of it—presided.

Three doors lead from the living room. Pippa opened the nearest one to see a big double bed monopolising the room, suits and shirts hanging in the open wardrobe. Treacherous thoughts and sensations flashed an image of waking up beside him, feeling his warm body next to hers.

"That's my room, and my bed."

Pippa looked back at him. What had he said? It was as though his words came at her muted, through the haze of images that clouded her senses.

"Where's my room?" She managed to get the words out of very tight lips as she backed away from his bedroom.

"This way." Jonathon crossed the living room to the opposite side and opened the door with a flourish. Man, he was sarcastic.

Thankfully, her room radiated calm and peace. A cream and grape quilt covered the queen double bed, with floor to ceiling built in wardrobes reflecting her image back to her. She stepped through a smaller open door to a shower room—gentle music piped through when she flicked the light switch. Best of all, she had access to the balcony, which stretched from her room past the living room and the master bedroom. It was to here she escaped, gratefully breathing in the sea air in the hope it would soothe her hot face and stop her mind on its relentless cycle: how would she share this space with a man who sent her senses fizzing alive just by being in the same vicinity as her? Working with Marcus had been hard, but nothing compared to this.

Her senses sharpened. The breeze wafted sea-salt through the air and she saw Jonathon stepping out of the living room to stand by her side. The irony of the situation nearly made her laugh aloud. Here they were, in one of the most romantic settings in the world, looking out as New Zealand slowly revealed itself. Yet the emotions that seethed between them, shifting and rolling, made her feel decidedly queasy. She couldn't even blame it on the sea, as she had always had perfect sea legs.

"It's a spectacular view, and I don't think I could ever get bored with the changing coastline." Jonathon raised an eyebrow as he looked at her.

Okay, in the name of diplomatic relations, she could do nice. Being nice was preferable to what had been going on previously between the two of them.

"It's wonderful, isn't it? I love hiking, or tramping as they call it here. I'm not sure how long it will take before the need to get out there overwhelms me."

"Are you often overwhelmed?"

To her dismay, Pippa felt her face growing hot in the sea air. She had never been one for blushing before—so why now?

"No, not really. It takes a lot to get to me." And why did she respond like that? Something had taken control of her tongue; she sounded like a flirt. Jonathon obviously thought so, for he swung around, resting his back against the balcony to look fully into her face.

"Are you sure?"

"Pardon?" More confusion. What was he saying now? Was her resolve under dispute? Did he think she'd fold as soon as something went wrong?

"Well, could I, for instance, get to you?" Uh-oh, he was flirting. And he was definitely getting to her. One minute he looked through her, the next he looked right into her very soul, making her feel she was new, fresh, and had been put on this earth for him and him only. A shiver ran through her, weakening her knees and sending a sparkle deep into her core.

She had to pull this back onto dry land. "I don't see why you'd want to, Mr. Eagleton. Not only am I just your chef, but also we happen to be sharing this suite for the next fourteen days. In the interest of diplomatic relations, I think we should perhaps try not to get to each other."

She caught a smile on his face as he turned back to view Mercury Island. "You can call me Jonathon, Pippa. And it's interesting you have to *try* not to let me get to you."

Not what she meant at all.

"Oh, you..." She stumbled to a halt and decided to leave before she said something she regretted. "I'm out of here." She turned back through the suite, wishing she could slam the door, but the hinge on the top of the door made it close an inch at a time. Slow enough for her to hear Jonathon's voice follow her through the cabin.

"I'm looking forward to my dinner tonight, thanks, Pippa."

Would he insist on needling her every time they met? Infuriating man. What had she ever done to deserve his lack of basic stranger's courtesy—where you assume people are nice until proven wrong?

Stop thinking about him, and start thinking about his menu instead. Nice and simple. Hot starter, chicken main, and dessert. For him and the little heiress.

Cooked well, indeed!

*

Jonathon remained out on the little balcony. Pippa had a good point: they were doomed to spend the next fourteen days in close quarters, so they should be adult about their relationship and ensure they got on. If he were being honest with himself, he didn't know what had gotten into him. Something irrepressible in him had enjoyed throwing little comments her way to see how she fielded them. She'd kept things above board, despite some goading.

He had enjoyed being out on the balcony with her, the sea breeze playing with her curls, and her green eyes changing to reflect the blue green of the sea. New Zealand would suit her very well, with the multitude of variations on blue and green, and all the shades in between. Pippa's flushes weren't disguised under foundation, but instead brought a glow to her face with her clear skin being shown off to its best advantage. She looked disingenuous when she flushed, cross when she delivered her barbed comments, but when she relaxed he found it hard to drag his eyes from her. The ever-present frown fading brought her face close to beauty, with her sparkling eyes, snub nose, and curved lips. She intrigued him.

Fine, he could admit that much to himself, but there was where the attraction, if that's what he could call it, stopped. Pippa Renshaw obviously used any means to progress her career—who knows, maybe she would decide that *he* was the one to seduce now Mulberry had been fired.

His iPhone rang, dragging him away from his dark thoughts. "Jonathon Eagleton."

"Jonathon, hiiiii, Juliet Stevenson." Her Texan accent drawled the words. "I'm just in my suite, and I wondered whether you could come and check something out for me? I'm in the Milford Suite."

"Oh? I hope everything is how you'd expect?"

Juliet expertly pitched her laugh, designed to get any red-blooded male's pulse beating faster. The sound only irritated him, overblown blondes not being his type.

"There's just one *teensy weensy* detail that I'm hoping you may be able to assist me with. Don't be long!" She hung up without waiting for an answer.

As he locked the door behind him, unease sank in his gut. Barely out of port and Juliet was already demanding special treatment. Unfortunately, her suite wasn't far away, and he soon found himself knocking on the Milford door.

"Door's open, darling, come on in. I'm on the balcony."

Making his way through the living room, he noted that Juliet seemed to have made herself at home. An open champagne bottle sat in a cooler, and the open bedroom door showed the bed already turned down.

When he stepped onto the balcony, he realised what a bad move he had made. Standing at the railing and clad in what seemed to be only a gold silk wrap, stockings, and high-heeled glass slippers, Juliet handed him a glass of champagne.

"Have a little drink, sweetie. Alcohol is good for sea legs, or so I hear." She smiled at him, whiter than white teeth gleaming.

"Thanks, Juliet." Jonathon took the glass. He had to get out of here, and fast. "So what can I do for you?" he asked, keeping his face carefully bland.

"Well, it's like this." Juliet took another drink from her champagne flute and Jonathon realised with an inward grimace she had been drinking already. "I love being out here on the balcony—I feel free. But the trouble is, the wind keeps playing with my wrap." As though to highlight her point, the wrap blew up, showing the tops of her lacy stockings. "I'll be cold, and I do hate being cold." She turned to him and playfully head butted his shoulder.

Was she mad? Exactly what did she think he'd do? Wrap his arms around her and shelter her from the elements? Hah, fat chance.

"Well, if I were you, Juliet, I would resort to putting some warmer clothes on."

She pouted, and he assumed she thought her pout a pretty one, whereas small wrinkles appeared around her small-pursed mouth. Impatience tied in with exasperation toward her.

"Surely you can come up with something better than that?"

Jonathon laughed, forcing the sound to be natural. He couldn't help comparing her to Pippa, to how fresh and free Pippa had looked in the sea breeze on their balcony. When the breeze touched Juliet's hair, it didn't move. He felt a touch on his sleeve and looked down to see the white tipped manicured nails rest on his bicep. Her hand gave a little squeeze, and he gently caught it and moved it away, ignoring the now dangerous glint in her blue eyes.

"You see, Jonathon, I know this is a deal clinching trip for you. Having our contract would considerably increase the worth of Queen Cruises, not to mention what the deal would do for your own career."

Jonathon inwardly sighed. He had known this trip spelt trouble, but he hadn't thought he'd have a seriously delusional woman to deal with.

"And what *I* want, Daddy wants too." Juliet stopped now, and took another sip of her drink.

Jonathon took the glass from her, disregarding the flare of passion in her eyes. He had to tread very carefully here. He needed her on his side. "Juliet, you're very sweet, but I really do think that drinking in the afternoon before you have acclimatised yourself to the movement of the ship may be a bit impractical." He kept his tone appropriately playful. "Now come inside, before you do get too cold." With this, he firmly grasped her elbow and pulled her back into the cabin. "I know you only flew in to Auckland this morning, so why not catch a few hours rest before the cocktails tonight, and don't forget that you and your family are dining in my suite at nine tonight."

"Oh, of course, I wouldn't want to ruin our dinner. And the cocktails, will you be there too?"

Jonathon said a prayer that his exasperation didn't show clearly on his face. "Of course I will, but I'll be working." Pushing her down on the sofa, he found a blanket to cover her. Thankfully, the combination of alcohol and jetlag were working together to induce a soporific stupor, and her eyelids dropped.

"I'll see you later."

Jonathon had nearly made good his escape before he heard her call out. "I do *love* a masterful man, Jonathon. Night-night."

*

Jonathon made his way quickly through the maze of corridors, his mind keeping up with the pace of his legs. Juliet knew very well what the Stevenson deal meant to him and to Queen Cruises, offering the opportunity to expand. But he hadn't counted on her making it clear that she was the deal clincher. He had to keep her sweet, but how to do that without appearing to succumb to her charms? Nearly cracking his head on a low doorframe— sometimes he hated the *compactness* of a cruise ship—he realised he had arrived at his office, and paperwork beckoned. At least it may distract him from the problem that was Juliet Stevenson. How was he going to manage her?

*

"This kitchen is a dream to work in." Pippa smiled over at Jean-Pierre, after spending the last hour prepping the food for main service in Corals restaurant that evening.

Jean-Pierre nodded back at her, pride in his glance. "We 'ave very dedicated staff 'ere. Christian, the kitchen porter, takes a lot of pride in this work. 'e also looks after the maintenance of ze appliances, and makes sure all is running smoothly for you. I also think that he will be a leedle bit in love with you, so will work even 'arder." At this, he gave a clap and a laugh, his eyes twinkling in merriment at the thought.

"Yes, I'm sure!" Pippa hoped her sarcasm wasn't lost on the French chef, as she didn't want him to think she was so immodest. But a quick glance at his good-natured face relaxed her.

"Jean Pierre, I'd like to ask your advice." Pippa had decided to check her menu with him, being that this was her first time cooking for the CEO. "Mr. Eagleton asked me for quite a basic menu: a hot starter, chicken main, and a dessert. So I thought to start with pan-fried scallops with warm tomato and avocado salsa, followed by baked chicken and pistachio pilaf with coconut, chili, and ginger sauce, fresh vegetables, and new potatoes. And to top the night off, white chocolate and berry cheesecake. What do you think? I want to do something classy for my first night."

"Mais oui, I like it. Would you like an 'and with it?"

"No, merci, Jean Pierre, I'll do it myself."

The hours flew by as Pippa flew around the kitchen, enjoying every minute as long as she didn't think too much about later that night—cooking for the CEO and his esteemed guests. Fiona popped her head around the kitchen door about six p.m. to see if Pippa wanted to join her for dinner at the staff canteen.

Pippa shook her head. "Thanks, Fiona, but I'll just grab something here." Nerves were stopping her from being hungry, but she didn't want to admit that, not even to her new friend.

The place started to get busy, with the waiting staff arriving full of good cheer for the first service of the cruise. Every time the out door to the restaurant swung open, Pippa heard cellos tuning amidst a low babble of voices. She paused, listening and loving the excitement palpable in the air. This was why she cooked. The tension before a busy service, the hard grafting during, and the relief and sheer tiredness afterwards. She thrived on it. And to have the opportunity to play with food all day long—heck, who wouldn't love her job?

She closed her eyes to give a good mental shake up inside and to get herself into top gear, ready to hit the ground running. She could do this. Upon opening them, she felt as though someone had thrown a bucket of seawater over her. In front of her, in full black tie—and what looked to be a black mood too—stood

Jonathon. She gasped, then tried to strangle it in a cough, and ended up sounding like a silly goose.

He scrubbed up well. The black tuxedo, clearly bespoke, moulded to his body and the shirt underneath with its soft folded collar had what must be a hand-tied burgundy bow tie, being ever so slightly off centre. The burgundy in the tie changed his tawny eyes to a molten gold, and the look they carried made her unsure whether her legs could sustain her anymore. After twenty-eight years of doing so, they were going to let her down now?

*

Jonathon forced himself not to stare. When he'd come through the kitchen door, Pippa had been standing there, eyes closed and before he knew it, his eyes feasted on the sight. The long dark lashes resting on high cheekbones, unruly curls pulled back in a high ponytail with an odd curl making a bid for freedom.

When her eyes opened, he watched with fascination the way her pupils widened to nearly block out all green and then pull back only a little so her big eyes dominated her face. The desire to reach out and kiss them gently shut, then trail kisses down to her rosebud mouth nearly overwhelmed him. How many freckles did she have scattered over her nose anyway?

"Mr. Eagleton, I mean Jonathon, I mean…oh I don't know what I mean." Pippa seemed thoroughly flustered now, and blew out an exasperated breath from pursed lips. Pursed *perfect* lips. The top buttons of her chef's whites were open, and her neck appeared long and graceful, plenty of room for lots of trailed kisses to lead down to her cleavage, and further…his throat went dry. What was he thinking? Annoyance shot through him as he realised he couldn't stop thinking about various parts of Pippa's body. So, she was beautiful, but he was her CEO, dammit. He shoved thoughts of Pippa from his mind, ignoring the protest of his tightening body.

"Daydreaming? As you seem to have lots of time on your hands, I would like to see the first draft of tomorrow's lunch menu when I come back after drinks with the guests." Good, the harsher the better to quell any other salacious thoughts.

Pippa looked down at his highly polished court shoes, and he saw her jawbone tighten. "Yes, of course, Mr. Eagleton, *sir.*"

She stood straight and he could've sworn she was about to salute him. Instead, she made an abrupt turn and walked off. Jonathon watched her go, unable to wrench his gaze from her.

Things weren't going to be quiet in this kitchen.

Or his suite.

Chapter Four

The closer Pippa got to nine p.m., the colder her blood ran. Her heart thumped erratically and the only way she could hold her nerves at bay was to put all her energy into preparing a melt-in-your-mouth meal for the evening. Still, her fingertips remained ice cold.

Time just ticked inexorably by.

As she clocked the waiters coming in to fetch the canapés for the cocktails, she wondered who to bring with her to serve her meal.

"Jean-Pierre!" she called out through the busy kitchen and went off to find him in the cold room checking on the desserts. "I'd like to take a waiter with me to serve, who would you recommend?"

Jean-Pierre shrugged in a typical Gallic way. "Bring Rob with you, 'e is very good. Rob!" Jean Pierre raised his voice and soon a young, attractive man of about twenty-five appeared. "Qui, Chef, what can I do for you?"

"Peepa needs an 'and serving M. Eagleton and 'is guests. Pleeze look after her."

Rob gave Pippa a nod. "I'd be delighted to, chef."

Pippa smiled at him, her shoulders already relaxing in the knowledge that she just needed to supervise.

Ready to start pan-frying the scallops, Pippa glared impatiently when Jonathon appeared at the door, holding it open with one hand to call over to her. "Sorry Pippa, we're running over time. It'll be at least nine forty-five before we sit down. Make sure the meal is nice and hot."

Pippa treated him to her best I-can't-believe-this-is-happening face.

He raised an eyebrow. "There's a good girl."

The door swung shut behind him before Pippa had time to vent her impatience. She clenched her hand shut, fingernails biting into her palm. Could he not have told her before now? And did he have to patronize her? She was damn good at her job. Nice and hot, my eye. Who did he think she was? A kitchen porter just starting out? Of course the dinner would be nice and hot. In fact, it could be *very* hot. The sauce contained chili, after all. But only for him. She could bake his in a separate dish, add an extra bit of chili to ensure a nice and hot dinner. She relaxed her hand, playing with the Claddagh ring on her baby finger.

There's a good girl. She harrumphed to herself as she re-heard his words.

Could she? Would she really dare to? Smiling to herself, she knew she'd love to, but perhaps in the interest of good relationships with her boss and roommate, she shouldn't really. But adding some chili would've been a lot of fun.

*

Jonathon walked back over to the Stevensons, grinning wryly to himself at the look on Pippa's face. As the string quartet played on, Jonathon thought surely his fake smile screamed lack of interest and still Juliet seemed blithely unaware of his indifference. She had walked into the bar like she was walking onto a yacht, ignoring all the eyes turned in her direction.

Either she knew how to act or she had been extremely drunk earlier on, for not by a blink of an eye did she let on they had met earlier. As the busy bar hummed in the background, Juliet kept demanding his attention by putting her hand on his forearm, leaning into him. Her overpowering scent of Opium threatened to herald a headache and he wished she would step even an inch away from him.

The other guests began to dissipate in search of dinner at any of the five restaurants on board. Only the Stevensons and another couple, the Bradley's were in the bar, a pair who were so sycophantic they nearly sickened Jonathon. Once they had heard the Stevensons were on board, they came over and attached themselves like limpets.

George Stevenson, Juliet's father, was very gracious and endured Mrs. Bradley's clumsy flirting with great equanimity. Nina, his wife, was less so but probably because the husband kept leering down her not-inconsiderable cleavage. They made an incongruous party, and glancing at his watch, Jonathon waited for a break in the conversation to galvanize the Stevensons for dinner. They were going to be really late unless they made a move now.

"Mr. and Mrs. Bradley, we must go to dinner now—"

He got no further, as Della Bradley squealed, "Oh we'd love to, wouldn't we, Barney?"

Jonathon hoped his grimace didn't show as he excused himself to tell Pippa the bad news.

"Pippa?" he called out as he came through the kitchen door. Despite being in the middle of service, the kitchen radiated calmness. Delicious smells hung in the air, and he checked the dinners ready to be served. They looked sumptuous and his stomach growled.

"Here," came the reply and when she made it obvious she wasn't coming to him, he sighed and went to find her. She was at the ovens, putting the tray of basted chicken in, absentmindedly blowing a stray curl from her face. He waited until she closed the oven door, shutting off the blast of hot air. The pot on the stove got her attention and she stirred it slowly, releasing the smell of ginger.

"We have two more guests for dinner, and we're heading up there now. Will you sort the extra meals out, please?"

She still didn't look up at him, and he didn't know what it was—exasperation, annoyance or just plain desire to get her to look at him—but something made him reach in and stick a baby finger into the sauce.

Now she was looking at him, askance on her face. He popped his finger in his mouth and sucked gently on it.

"Delicious, but perhaps it could be a bit spicier, please, chef." Out of his peripheral vision, he saw her flinch and he deemed a fast exit appropriate.

"Yes, sir." Her words were clearly spoken through clenched teeth and he smiled to himself. Was that sarcasm he heard in her voice? Her head was bent low, so he couldn't see her expression. Too bad if it was sarcasm. This being the catering industry, you had to be prepared for the unexpected. If she couldn't handle it, then she wouldn't make the grade for head chef.

"Fine, see you up there."

*

The goddamn *cheek* of the man, sticking his finger in her work. Urgh. She placed the sauce pot in the sink and ran water into it to disperse it down the plug hole. Starting from scratch, because there was absolutely no way she would serve that now.

"Rob?" Pippa raised her voice, looking for her helper. She stalked into the cold room and gathered the ingredients anew, mind working furiously. A bit spicier, hey. She'd give him spicy. Her hands flew whilst chopping the ginger and she moved onto the chili, glancing at her watch. She had to work fast.

Without stopping to think, she chopped more chili and, after placing most of the ingredients into a main pot for all of the other guests, started a small pot. *Especially* for Jonathon. A little bit spicier indeed. Take that!

There. Done. No turning back now, although a remote part of her stood apart with crossed arms saying, *What the hell are you doing?*

"I'm here, chef." Rob materialized beside her, looking over at her with bemusement. Pippa straightened her face with an effort. "I need to you move lightning fast, get up to the Doubtful, and add an extra two seats at the table. We have another two guests, and they are moving up there now. So you need to be quick. I'll send the starters up in the lift as soon as the extra two are done. Now shoo!"

"Okay, great. I'll let you know when I'm clearing the starter." Rob's voice tapered out as he disappeared in the direction of the exit.

Pippa concentrated on frying more scallops—two seconds extra frying and they would be ruined. She hummed distractedly, refusing to think of what she'd done. The only thoughts in her head was "spicier please." The brazen look on his face, gold flecks in his eyes just daring her to react to him.

Her mouth watered as the smell of frying scallops rose, reminding her she hadn't had anything to eat yet. Pushing her hunger to the back of her mind, she loaded the butler's tray and sent it up in the lift to Rob.

Don't think just do.

The chicken sizzled nicely, and she tasted the sauce for the Stevensons. The pistachios added a lovely, almost toasted almonds taste, the chili stayed in the background only to linger on her tongue after she swallowed, and the taste of the coconut soothed the flavours down.

Perfect. *For some maybe.*

The food lift pinged its arrival, giving her heart a little jumpstart. Nearly dropping the dishes in her hurry to get them away from her, she loaded up the main course and sent it on its way.

He deserves it, remember.

But would she deserve getting sacked?

Rationale finally managed to break through into her hothead.

Damn what had she done? Groaning audibly, she flung her chef's towel from her and left the kitchen at a run. Maybe she could get there in time to stop Rob serving. She huffed up the stairs and followed the long corridor around to the suites. Who knew it was so far from the kitchens?

As she opened the door to the suite, she heard a peal of laughter, followed by a gaggle of voices. Piano music played in the background and the soft glow from the chandelier warmed the room. A balmy sea breeze blew through the doors, wafting around the suite to release the smell of roses from the display on the sideboard.

All at odds with the jangling alarm in her veins.

Jonathon glanced up from his conversation, tawny eyes warm as he smiled at her. She flashed him a quick smile, looking at the table to see what was in front of the guests. *Of course.* The main course was out, complete with sauce.

"Ah, good. Everyone, this is our new superb head chef of Corals, Pippa Renshaw. For our good fortune, we have her cooking solely for us tonight. Pippa, let me be the first to congratulate you on the scallops, the flavours were wonderfully intense, and an excellent way to start our meal. Well done."

Pippa blinked. Had she heard right? Was he actually complimenting her? There were murmurs of agreement from the other guests. What was he going say after trying the main course? Perhaps she could rescue his plate yet.

"Yes, Jonathon daaarling, you are right. Of course." The American accent broke through Pippa's confusion, and she nearly looked twice when she saw Juliet sitting by Jonathon's right hand side. Her features were so familiar, Pippa felt she was looking at a friend of hers. Not that any friend of hers would look back with such contempt. Clearly, Juliet didn't expect to hobnob with the *staff.*

Her hand lay on Jonathon's forearm, fingers splayed possessively as though she never intended to let go. Adopting the critical eye Pippa employed in looking over her dishes, she could see that they made a very attractive couple. Juliet, with her overly done good looks, and Jonathon, with his understated charisma, were perfect foils for each other. *Easy, tiger, anyone would think you cared.* Her nerves for the evening dissolved, replaced by a dull emptiness.

"I'm glad you enjoyed it." Pippa managed to get the words out from a tight throat. "I hope you enjoy the rest too. Can I get you anything else?" But out of her peripheral vision, she saw him take a mouthful of his main course. She turned to look fully at him as he hesitantly swallowed and coughed, tears coming to his eyes.

Juliet's voice sounded sweet as sugar. "Oh, darling, did it go down the wrong way? Here, have some of my water." Taking advantage of the situation, she draped her arm around his shoulder as he quietly coughed some more. She glared at Pippa. "Or maybe it's poisonous. Perhaps your *wonderful* chef isn't so wonderful. Here, let me take a taste."

She raised a fork.

Pippa's stomach twisted. Jonathon's eyes met hers, and she was sure he could see her plea. *Don't let her try it!*

"Juliet!" Her mother's voice rang out through the room. "Your behaviour is appalling. What is the matter with you?"

Pippa's stomach unclenched. Her future on board wasn't looking good as it was, never mind the disaster that would ensue if Juliet had tried the hot sauce.

The sweet, caring look that had been predominant on Juliet's face turned into a pettish, childish snarl. "You insisted I come along on this forsaken tin boat, *I* didn't want to. So you can hardly take it out on me just because I'm looking for a bit of fun whilst I'm stuck here." She flounced back in her seat and took a gulp from her wine glass, emptying it. With a flick of her wrist, she gestured to it, and raised her eyebrows imperiously at Rob, who, exemplary waiter that he was, complied.

Although Pippa didn't like scenes, she was glad the heat had been taken from Jonathon's reaction to her sauce. Looking at him now, she saw him dabbing at his mouth with his serviette in a vain attempt to hide the curling of his lip. The heat from the chili seemed to have reached his eyes as they slowly simmered under his thick lashes. They turned a deep whisky brown and the gold in them glittered dangerously. Almost as though he turned the heat on her, her face started to warm up.

"This is excellent also, Pippa."

Had she misheard? "Pardon?"

"I very much like this sauce, although I'm not sure what the predominant ingredient is. Is it the chili, the coconut, or maybe even the ginger? In fact please, just to humour me, I'd like you to take a taste, savour the sauce and tell me the flavours you taste." He looked at the Stevensons. "This is the beauty of having the chef come to the table. You get to ask questions about how your dinner was made."

"Oh." Pippa had a sneaking feeling she looked like a fish with her mouth fallen open. "I wouldn't dream of trying yours. I'll fetch another sauce from the kitchen."

"Too right," Juliet murmured, words nearly blocked out by her wine glass close to her lips.

"No, not at all, please, try mine." Jonathon dipped his dessert spoon into his sauce and held it out to her, heavily loaded. Juliet straightened up, and her eyes took him in, then flew to Pippa. The scene looked like a caricature of two lovers sharing a dish, and Juliet's eagle eyes spotted it.

"Um, thanks." Pippa took the spoon and, mentally blocking her nose to save herself from some of the heat, swallowed the sauce.

"Savour the flavors," Jonathon almost crooned at her, his eyes now showing nothing but merriment. "Now, what can you taste? No, don't spoil the taste with water, tell us all about the prominent one."

Pippa felt as though her mouth was on fire. "As you rightly pointed out, Jonathon, the chili is the prominent flavour, with after tones of ginger." The chili burst into her mouth and the quantity made her feel as though flames were about to emerge. She had always wanted to be a dragon when she was growing up. "Followed swiftly by the soothing coconut."

"Thank you, Pippa." Jonathon held his wine glass up to her; to all the others it looked as though he were praising her, but she knew better. He held the glass up as though to say, *We're even, you and I. Don't even think about trying that again.*

She tilted her head to the side, and gave a half smile in return. Fair enough. She couldn't complain.

*

The memory of what Pippa had done kept Jonathon amused for the rest of the evening, which passed by without a hitch.

The Bradleys reluctantly left after Della fell asleep at the table, citing jetlag rather than her copious consumption of the very good Chablis Premier Cru. Nina's comment to Juliet seemed to have taken the wind out of her sails, for she too soon yawned and hinted loudly at Jonathon to walk her back to her suite. George threw his eyes exasperatedly up to heaven.

"Don't mind my daughter, Jonathon, it's just the jet lag talking." The look he gave his daughter made it clear he thought the world of her. "Come on, sweetheart, Daddy will take you home." Putting her hand over her yawning mouth, Juliet stood and swayed. George grabbed her before she could fall into Jonathon's arms, and Nina stood too.

"Thank you for a very enjoyable evening. We're very much looking forward to seeing White Island tomorrow."

Jonathon bid them good night, and called down for the room service staff to come and clear away. He sat at the table, nearly empty wine glass in his hand. He couldn't believe the evening that had passed. The impudence of Pippa, lacing his sauce. His heart had nearly stopped when he had tasted the chili, and he had been on the verge of warning George not to eat the sauce, but he was too late.

However, the look of delight on George's face reassured him. Obviously, his sauce was the only one laced. He chuckled to himself, then stopped. If the waiting staff came in to find him laughing alone at the dinner table, all his hard-won credibility would be lost. He pushed his chair back to stand when the door opened.

"Knock before coming in, please, in the future." He couldn't have the staff just walking in, even if he had called them.

"Certainly, then I'll ask you to do the same." Pippa's voice sounded cool, her English accent familiar after the evening spent with the Americans, but her face belied the coolness. Her eyes lightened to a spearmint color and looked suspiciously glassy, with her rosebud mouth all but disappeared into a long line. Even her freckles seemed to have paled.

"I thought you were the staff, come to clear up."

"Well, you're right there, I *am* the staff, just not coming to clear up, rather to catch some sleep. I'm quite tired." Pippa's voice faltered and she crouched down to tie up shoelaces, which, from his view point, didn't need tying up.

"Are you okay?" Jonathon reached out to her. He gazed down at the tumble of curls, watching them shake, followed by her shoulders doing the same. His heart expanded, and without stopping to think, he hunkered down beside her. He hooked his finger under her chin to lift her face up. By now, tears were streaming down her face, and she kept her eyes shut rather than look at him, her dark thick lashes clumped together, failing to hold the tears in. Pulling her up, he threw caution to the wind and engulfed her in a bear hug. Maybe he could just will her tears away. A little voice wondered what the hell he was doing.

"I'm just...just..." The words ended on a wail.

"It's okay, it's okay." Jonathon murmured the words to her, shocked by the feelings whirling in him caused by Pippa in his arms. How could she fit so well? Her head reached the crook of his neck, with her face turned inwards under his chin. A lean and fit body warmed his, curves pressed against his chest, and slim arms around his back. Smelling her hair, he caught the scent of fresh lavender despite the hours spent in the kitchen.

"Jetlagged…and tired…and homesick…" Pippa punctuated each word with a sniff, then buried her head deeper into his neck.

A noise like thunder broke through Jonathon's consciousness and the door to the suite swung open, with Rob coming through first, pulling a trolley. Jonathon cursed to himself as he pulled Pippa's arms from around him and they took a step back from each other. An inaudible groan escaped Jonathon's lips, as he realized how this must look to the staff. A glance at Pippa confirmed his fears, for guilt radiated from her pale face.

Rob, on the other hand, went bright red. "Sorry, sir, sorry." He muttered the words whilst chewing his lip.

"Oh hi, Rob, you must have come to clear up?" Pippa visibly tried to pull herself together, scrabbling for a tissue in her pocket to wipe her eyes.

"Yeah, Mr. Eagleton just phoned down and asked for some staff up here."

"I'll give you a hand."

Jonathon cleared his throat to take control. "No, no Pippa, you're exhausted from jetlag and the understandable stress of your first evening. You need a good night's sleep." He *had* been about to tell her to go to bed but he didn't want to say anything that may be misconstrued; the situation was already awkward enough. "I'll help here."

"Well, if you're sure then." The strain on Pippa's face seemed to shift, and she looked very young all of a sudden. Jonathon nodded at her, endeavouring to keep his face blank. She looked so vulnerable and all he wanted right now was to protect her.

"You were great tonight, the Stevensons waxed lyrical about your food, so don't worry. I'm sure it's only jetlag and perhaps you were a little overwhelmed after your first day working on the other side of the world." He crooked an eyebrow, happy to see a small smile, albeit a weary one, appear on her face.

Pippa nodded, and saying goodnight to them both, retired to her bedroom. The click on the door left Jonathon in no doubt the door was locked.

"Pippa did extremely well tonight." Jonathon worked hard to keep his voice level. Dammit, he, the new CEO, had been found in a totally compromising situation with one of his staff.

"It was a pleasure working with her." Rob kept his head down, clearing the table.

"She was under a great deal of pressure. I think she ended up feeling a bit overwhelmed." Jonathon watched Rob, wondering how much more he had to say. Rob stopped tidying, and straightened up to look at him, his gaze direct and open.

"I like chef, she was great to work with tonight and I want to carry on working with her. The staff in her kitchen seem to be taking to her too. Anyway, there's really no need to help me clear up, I'll be out of here in a jiffy."

He nodded. He couldn't do more now, for to say anything else would only draw attention to them. Pouring a shot of whisky from the decanter, he stepped through the double doors onto the balcony. How could he have let this happen? He had thought to avoid a compromising situation with Juliet, never thinking that it would be with Pippa instead.

How would this look to all the staff tomorrow morning? They would think he was just another Mulberry. Staff morale flat lined at a record low. How would the employees feel now, thinking that yet another Jack-the-lad headed up the company? And if that wasn't bad enough, there was still the small problem of Juliet. He took deep breaths, and focused on the positive.

Rob seemed to have understood what Jonathon intimated, but even so. He was sure to tell his close friends what with both Jonathon and Pippa being new and in senior roles.

Dammit.

Working in such a close environment made it hard enough to inspire staff loyalty without all this blowing up in his face.

Chapter Five

Standing with her back against the door, Pippa felt as though she had hit rock bottom. Only two short hours ago, she had been on top of the world. She had risen to the challenge and cooked up a good impression, and had been congratulated on it. Perhaps it was the congratulatory champagne that had done it. She'd only had half a glass, but combine that alcohol with her jetlag, being homesick, nerves over a new job, home *and* boss and who could blame her emotions for running wild.

To top it all off, the aftermath of her trick—her desire to get back at Jonathon, swiftly followed by disbelief that she had done it—had left her feeling flat. When he had barked the order to knock before entering their shared cabin, it had been the final straw.

The floodgates had opened. He had been incredibly gentle with her, though, and in his arms, a feeling of calmness crept into her, the quiet before the storm. Her homesickness had transformed into a sense of belonging that she had never felt before. A sense that had started to morph and swirl deep within her, bringing all her nerve points to the points where her body touched his. Control over herself, her mind, her emotions all weakened and she would've melted into him, had Rob not entered when he did. Why?

Sure, he was big, strong, and handsome, but she had been with similar men, none of whom had produced such a profound response in her. What would it be like to be kissed by him? A shiver ran through her as the image of Jonathon lowering his head to kiss her invaded her thoughts.

Madness. This was a man she had met scarcely twenty-four hours ago.

Thank God they had been interrupted. Who knows what would've happened? If he had felt the same—impossible to think—but just say he had. This was taking it to the extreme, sure, but how would she be feeling now after once more having sex with the boss? Especially as the boss seemed to think she had no problem with sleeping her way to the top.

A tinkling of glass interrupted her fervent thanks. Rob and Jonathon were talking in low voices. Hearing her name mentioned, and despising herself even as she was doing so, Pippa pressed her ear against the door. Fragments of the conversation came to her. *Pressure...* At this she pressed her ear to the door even more tightly. *Overwhelmed...carry on working...*

Pippa pulled herself away from the door and cursed herself for listening in the first place. On autopilot, she got changed and into bed to huddle in a fetal position. A multitude of thoughts besieged her. Just moments ago, she had been talking herself into fancying a man who obviously had just been trying to calm her down. Fair enough, she may be attracted to him—but there was no way he reciprocated that attraction. He was just protecting his ship. Her stomach dipped, and she closed her eyes wearily.

Jeez, she could be such a fool sometimes.

Her inundated mind started whirling, reproducing flash images.

Saying goodbye to her parents. The flight.

Meeting Jonathon.

Jonathon raising a glass in sardonic humour.

Being in Jonathon's arms.

Standing against the door, hearing Jonathon talk about her.

The last three stuck on a relentless loop, drawing tears from behind her closed eyes and they stayed in her mind when sleep finally came to claim her.

*

The Coral Princess berthed the next morning at White Island. The motion of the ship slowing was what finally woke Pippa, and despite feeling drained, she threw back the covers to head onto the balcony to see the island for herself.

The air smelt of the acrid smoke that the active volcano constantly produced. From her vantage point, Pippa could see the yellow and white crystals in the grey rock. It was bleak but beautifully so.

She drank in the view, exhilarating in not being able to see one single man-made structure on the island. It was pure nature, just the way it always had been. Lucky her, cruising around New Zealand *and* being paid for it. Energised, she showered in her en-suite and made her way to the kitchen, a smile in her eyes.

"Bonjour, Peepa, 'ow are you?" Jean-Pierre looked up from the sauce he was stirring on the gas hob.

"Great, thanks, Jean-Pierre, and how are..." Pippa's voice stumbled to a halt as it was clear Jean-Pierre wasn't listening, rather he was gazing at his sauce with a small frown.

"This eezn't working!" He lifted the pot from the hob to see there was no flame underneath. "Christian? Christian!"

An answering shout of "I'm coming" echoed through the kitchen, and the redheaded Christian ran past the cool rooms to him, toolkit in hand.

"I know, chef, it's not working anywhere in the kitchen from what I gather. I'll head to the point of intersection, and see if the rest of the ship is supplied."

"'urry up, please. We only 'ave two hours to prepare our à la carte and we can't do it without the cooking!"

Christian disappeared, and Jean-Pierre took off his chef's hat and flung his kitchen towel over his shoulder.

He held an arm out to Pippa. "We need to wait to see what 'e finds. Come, let us get a coffee." He put his hand on the small of Pippa's back and directed her toward the coffee machine. If she needed yet another excuse to love her job, constant good quality coffee on tap would do the trick.

"Thanks, Jean-Pierre. Has this ever happened before?"

"Neever. I know not what we will do." He shrugged, and taking a sip of coffee, tried to hide his worried face. The kitchen behind them slowly ground to a halt as the chefs gathered in groups, confusion showing on their faces.

"Well," said Pippa, "if the other kitchens are still fed by gas, perhaps they can help?"

"Not possible, I'm sorry. Zay are too small to cope, and also, is too far away from the restaurant."

Rob approached the two of them, the dismal expression on his face doing nothing to allay their fears. "Christian has just been on the phone—he says all the other departments are fine, it's only our kitchen that's out. The engineers are being called out but it will take a few hours before they arrive."

"Merde." Jean Pierre looked askance at Pippa. "Sorry, Peepa, very sorry. Alors! What shall we do?"

Pippa absentmindedly fiddled with her Claddagh ring, and caught her bottom lip between her teeth. "So, we can't cook anything here. Let's just do a cold buffet, and shift the lunch à la carte menu to dinner time, to avoid wasting the ingredients. The sun is shining, and the guests won't know any better. I know you said the other kitchens can't help, but I'm sure they can cook some meats for us."

Jean Pierre looked at her, chewing on his lip. "I think you are right. You ask each of the other three kitchens to cook some chicken, beef and 'am. It will not be much but is something. There are only seventy-nine booked in, we can close the book. We can do it as long as we're fast." Reaching out, he squeezed Pippa's cheek the way he would a baby, and chuckled. "To work then, ma biche." He took off walking at a thousand miles an hour.

The kitchen buzzed back to life: the sound of the washing machine nearly drowning out the scattered conversation and laughter that flowed through the fluorescent-lit kitchen as the chefs got down to business. The apprehension of whether they'd be able to make an entire cold menu look attractive hung in the air.

Pippa kept her head down, overseeing the starters and desserts. She put the four chefs working under her through their paces, questioning them for their ideas on what to do without gas. They had some bright ideas, which, after she spent a few minutes with each, they tweaked to sound mouth-wateringly delicious. There was a focused hum in the air surrounding her and her chefs as they got down to work, the odd joke being bantered around their station.

Pressure suited her, for her mind found a cool clarity in working hard, no margin for error. She worked fast, chopping, slicing, tasting, mixing, only pausing now and then for a quick drink of water. Life was nice and simple.

The smell of sea pines faintly mixed with spices came to her, and she shook her head slightly, confused, for it was certainly the first time she had ever smelt spring onions like that, only to slowly become aware of a presence beside her. *His* presence, more to the point. The suite had been empty when she had left, and she had forgotten the charismatic presence that she was finding increasingly magnetising. She glanced up to the right to see Jonathon watching her hands work.

"You move fast," he commented. The weariness she had woken with threatened to return. Dear God, what was he referring to now? Move fast in what respect? Ending up in his arms last night? Oh, it was just all too confusing and it was *she* who made it so. She cast another fervent thanks that Rob had entered their suite when he had. Deciding on a non-committal reply, she nodded. "We are busy."

"So I see."

"Any news on when the gas will return?"

"The engineers are here, so we're hoping to be up and running by three p.m. How are you today?" His voice had lowered, and he leaned in closer to her. If she didn't know any better, he sounded as though he cared.

"Yes, yes, fine, thank you. I do apologise for crying all over your suit last night. A glass of champagne seemed to have sent me over the edge—it won't happen again." As she endeavoured to sound matter of fact, she neatly sliced the nail on her right hand thumb. A rookie mistake, when was the last time that had happened? Had he seen? Did he know the effect he had on her, standing so close to her? The shakes came to her legs and before they reached her hands for all to see, she reached around him for the next batch of herbs to chop, giving him her best "back-off-outta-my-space" look.

"Oh, but champagne is a tradition on the last night of the cruise for all hard-working staff. I hope you'll reconsider." His tone was serious, but he didn't take the hint. She glanced at him, his broad shoulders outlined against the light behind him. Mistake. His open-necked white shirt showed a smattering of hair and outlined his defined pecs. What would they feel like under her hands?

Concentrate, Renshaw, concentrate.

"I mean about the cry…" Pippa's voice died away as she realised that he was teasing her. Flustered, she returned her gaze to her chopping board, only to peek up sideways at him under her eyelashes, amused at being caught out. And, okay, she admitted to herself, to see his smile again, to see his eyes crinkle in enjoyment at their exchange. She was enjoying it herself.

Overwhelmed suddenly came into her mind, and their brief chat drained of its pleasure. Of course, he's just making sure she's not as overwhelmed as she was last night. Last night! Her realisation that there was something about this man that pulled her in, rendering her powerless. Had she been overreacting? She shut her eyes briefly, looking inside herself, to witness her inner turmoil. Yet he was blithely unaware of it.

All *he* wanted was to make sure she didn't jump ship.

There was *she*, fantasising about his lips.

Ha. Would she never learn? Rejection settled like a curled up snake in the pit of her stomach.

"Is there anything you want?" Turning to look at him full on, she knew her tone sounded curt, but her throat threatened to close in and she could barely get her words out. Damn. She sounded like a harpy. Could it get any worse? Misery dampened her senses, mist rolling in to cover the hills. He must only think the worst of her, how could he think otherwise? In the past forty-eight hours—was that all it was?—he had seen her annoyed, confused, upset, and now a harpy. Great.

His tawny eyes narrowed as he took in her face. Almost imperceptibly, he nodded. "Just checking everything is okay in the kitchen. Good work, carry on, Pippa. I look forward to seeing the results laid out." So he was back to patronising. Pippa could handle that, far better to be patronised than to be flirted with.

Much safer.

She watched him leave. Even the way he walked away was attractive. Straight back, sublime shoulders tapering in to a slim waist, his high, curved backside begging out for her hand to caress it. How did he manage to get his trousers to fit so well?

Pippa breathed in, breathed out, repeated it, and concentrated on her food. Normally, once she turned her attention to her creating, everything else took a back seat.

Not this time.

*

Pippa was right, the girl was absolutely right, Jonathon found himself thinking as he walked away from Pippa. Obviously, she saw fit to maintain a distance between them at all times. He had decided after the fiasco with Rob last night to avoid speaking with her unless totally necessary. If Rob was spreading stories about them, steering clear of her was the only way to ensure that those who heard the rumours disbelieved them.

So actively seeking her out to talk to her didn't quite fit in with his decision, but there had been no one else around at the time, and he couldn't resist a little jibe in order to see her smile this morning. The way she had looked sideways at him was such a flirty look, it still sent honey thickening his veins. His mind lingered on her, the way her hair had fallen over her forehead, meeting her lashes, between which a bright glimmer of green had peeked mischievously. Captivating. His pelvis tightened involuntarily as he envisaged her looking at him like that, and him having the freedom to take it further. See what her mischief led to. Pippa trailing kisses down his naked torso, pausing only to look up at him with *that* look, then carrying on down… His mouth drained of saliva, and his heart thumped erratically. He stopped at a counter and put his hand out to steady himself. Breathe. Breathe, dammit, stop the blood heading straight between his legs, before anyone expected anything coherent from him. He gritted his jaw. Think of the money, that seven million…where could it have gone?

Breathe.

Okay. And *don't* think of Pippa.

He saw Jean-Pierre behind the service counter, switching off the lights that kept hot food warm.

He went over to him. "All under control, I see, Jean-Pierre?"

"Qui, monsieur, we are all fine." Jean-Pierre looked at him with something akin to pride in his face. "That leedle girl, that Peepa, she is *vraiment* good. She es even better than me!" He threw up his hands in mock horror. "Ze problem this morning was no problem to 'er. She 'as a talent for her food, and I 'ave no worrees in leaving this kitchen to 'er."

Jonathon looked at him. "Coffee?"

"Always." Jean-Pierre nodded and walked with him over to the coffee station. He tutted when he saw all the group heads in place, filled with used coffee. Taking two out, he banged them against the knockout box below the machine, refilled them with freshly ground coffee, and set them back in place over two cups. "Peepa, she 'as it all in 'er control. I like her, Monsieur Eagleton, eef only I was ten years younger!" He pressed a button on the machine and it hummed into life.

Jonathon couldn't figure out whether Jean-Pierre had been speaking to Rob, and if the rumours had begun. The smell of coffee rose, and he inhaled appreciatively.

Just what he needed, another stimulant after the heady stimulation of Pippa.

He quickly shut her image out, but her name remained on his lips. "Do you think Pippa will cope with working on a cruise ship?"

"Mais oui, why not?" He handed Jonathon his coffee. "I know is 'ard, living and working on a ship, but I think Peepa is full of fun. She es enthusiastic, but unlike most, does not use enthusiasm to 'ide a lack of knowledge or personality. I think everyone will like to work with her. You agree, non?"

Jonathon strove for a non-committal reply. Great, she was liked. Well, why wouldn't she be? She was…wonderful. He kept his face straight as his stomach crashed. This couldn't happen. Not in his company, not after Mulberry.

"Well, I'll know at the end of this cruise. She seems to be shaping up well."

"Yes, oui, shaping up well." There was an innocent look to Jean-Pierre's face that told Jonathon he *had* been talking to Rob. He was going to have to be very careful to avoid being seen with her. Slapping the other man on the back, he nodded his thanks and headed up to his office, armed with his caffeine fix.

It took a lot to impress Jean-Pierre, and Jonathon was torn between gratitude that Mulberry's white elephant seemed to be the surprise of the cruise, and regret that he had no way to get her off the ship. For if it was a case of his name being dragged through the mud or getting Pippa off the ship, Jonathon would have no choice but to find her a different ship. He hadn't worked his butt off since he was sixteen to achieve his goal, only to have Pippa bring it crashing down around his ears.

But he could control this situation.

He would stop thinking about Pippa, especially in compromising situations with him and no one else, maybe in a hot shower or a cool breeze skittering over her skin as she lay butt naked on his bed, glancing up at him with those bright eyes darkened in desire.

Dammit.

He had to avoid her at all times, and when he couldn't avoid her, he couldn't engage with her.

Two rules. He was CEO and could follow two petty rules, dammit.

Just think of Mulberry, and the unpleasant circumstances surrounding Pippa's interview.

A little niggle swam in his tummy, but disappeared before he could grasp it to understand it.

*

Pippa walked through the now quiet kitchen, checking to make sure it gleamed. The cold buffet had gone down well with the guests, and the gas had been fixed and was ready for dinner service. It was nice to have the place to herself—her stomach still flipped at the thought that it was her kitchen. In about half an hour or so, the chefs and kitchen staff would return, bringing the place back to life. She ran a finger over the stainless steel counter, ensuring it was clean when the door from the staff corridor shushed open and Fiona came through.

"Pippa…what are you up to?"

"Just finishing up here, why?" Pippa looked at her friend with a big smile on her face. Misery could be kept at bay when you had fun with a new friend.

"We're docking at Whangara, you know, where they made the movie *Whale Rider*. There's a traditional Maori cultural experience on and a few of us are going. Are you working tonight?"

"Now that I know the run of this place, there's really no need for both head chefs to be here, and Jean-Pierre has said that as he's leaving the ship when we reach Akaroa, he'll cover tonight. So great, I have the night off! Perfect timing, hey!"

"Get you, girl, you've already got the Kiwi accent, hey!" Fiona teased Pippa. "Although your pale English skin couldn't be mixed up with the Maori skin. They're so tanned and just so—oh—handsome, and capable, and strong, and..." Fiona was obviously looking forward to the evening.

"Fiona!" Pippa laughed at her. "Is David not coming?"

"Ah yeah." Fiona's Irish accent got stronger. "Sure he knows I love him to bits, and just like the odd look, that's all! No problem there, he knows me well enough by now."

"Okay, I'll run and get changed and see you at the Xplorer to go ashore."

"Be quick," warned Fiona. "The boat leaves the ship in forty minutes."

Pippa ran back to the Doubtful, sure it would be empty. It was late afternoon, Jonathon was bound to be doing something all CEO-ish.

She pushed open the heavy door, only to stop up short as she noticed the doors open to the balcony, with the curtains swaying in the breeze. Jonathon must have forgotten to close them. The fresh sea air was invigorating.

Showering in no time at all, she changed into a pair of combat trousers and hesitated about putting a cardigan on over her white peasant top. It looked like a lovely sunny day outside, but it could be quite chilly. Going out her balcony door to check, she came up short to see Jonathon leaning over the balcony railings, looking deep in thought.

"Oh sorry, I didn't realise you were here." Pippa cursed to herself for not realising. She wouldn't have come out if she had known he was there, cardigan or not. She didn't need any further onslaught on her senses.

"That's fine." Jonathon didn't look at her. "Although I notice you didn't knock when you came in." At this his head turned to take her in, his eyes a slate brown, lips set in a straight line.

"I thought you'd be working." Pippa felt forced to justify herself.

"I am." His face was so devoid of humour that Pippa's insides felt as though she had just swallowed a large slush puppy in a hurry.

"Well, why don't I just leave again, that way you can stop working." Pippa turned on her heel and, going back through her room, exited the suite. If that was his attitude, well, that suited her down to the ground. She didn't care, why should she? Obviously, he didn't see the need to ensure that she wasn't overwhelmed anymore. That must be a compliment. Oh, what the heck, she was spending far too much time thinking about him anyway.

It would be good to put some distance between them.

Chapter Six

As she stepped from the Xplorer, Pippa stretched and quashed the desire to lie on the ground. After being on an unstable medium, nothing felt better than solid earth beneath her feet. And Whangara, where they had docked, was special. The beach curled and hugged the green hills, providing a glorious contrast to the hues of the sea, which crashed into shore only to shuck back over the sand.

A girl could lose herself here.

The shadows grew as darkness fell, reducing the hills to a mysterious silhouette, and the fires on the beach sent seeking fingers of jagged flames crackling upwards. Pippa pinched herself as she sat just out of the circle of campfire light. She wanted to soak it all in before rejoining her friends. The Maori were in traditional dress, the men in kilt-like skirts with a wide belt and a cape, and the women dressed similarly, some of them with grass skirts. They had been speaking and chanting in the Maori tongue all throughout the evening as they cooked their food in a hole in the ground surrounded by hot stones—a *hangi*—and served the strong, thick home brew. Their beating of the drums provided an ever-present background rhythm that Pippa swayed automatically to.

Smelling the heady scent of joss sticks from several that were rooted in the earth, the memory of the one time she had smoked marijuana came to her. This was a similar feeling to being stoned, in that she didn't know quite what was going on, and the feeling of being overwhelmed was never far away. Fiona was up dancing with David and the others in Maori style, and Pippa watched from the fringe, the flickering of the fire barely lighting her up.

As she caught a wreath of smoke in her gaze, she followed it up into the indigo night sky, and her eyes widened yet again at the sight of so many stars. The Southern Cross emblazoned the night sky, sparkling like diamonds on a velvety indigo background, and the Milky Way showered the night sky in swathe after swathe of sprinkled stars. She leant back on her elbows to watch the stars dance, holding her face up, smelling the briny air as the sea breeze gently blew over her.

But the beat of the drum didn't allow her to disappear into her thoughts, pulling her back instead to the here and now. Maori dancers encircled their group, whooping and calling to each other in their strange sounding dialect. How did Fiona describe them? Strong, capable, handsome. She sure had that one right. They came closer. One of them, strange and fierce looking with dark makeup streaking his face, threw out a hand and pulled her up to dance. Pippa wanted to yank herself out of his grasp, but he wouldn't let her go without a struggle. Her heart in her mouth, she gave herself up to the music.

A celebratory dance, it was one performed throughout the centuries when the hunters returned victorious. In the midst of all the swirling, bowing, and whooping, Pippa's hair freed itself from the constricting tie and she shook her head in sheer light-headiness. The beat of her heart matched the beat of the drums. She followed her partner and swooped down to the earth, swung back to the sky, flung her arms open toward the sea, and again. The repetition made it into one fluid motion down, back, open. Time stood still while Pippa's veins flooded with dissolved stardust, bringing exhilaration coursing through her. The primal movement came naturally to her and she lost herself.

Her eyes opened of their own accord to fall onto a single standing shadow. The fire leapt higher, and a face was etched in light for a flickering second, showing tawny eyes watching her steadily with a dark look of desire. Pippa felt a lightning shaft of energy run through her body—*Jonathon was watching*—and she danced with revamped energy, her body moving for him, and him only. The beat of the drums found an answer in the throbbing in her pelvis, a liquid, warm pulsing. Her eyes closed, and her head filled with shadows and light and longing. The drums went faster, faster still, until the moon, stars, fire, light merged into a swirling spinning top, round and round. A final loud beat and the drums fell silent, allowing the dancers to fall, spent, onto the ground.

"Wasn't that just the best feeling ever?" Fiona collapsed beside her, panting and red faced from her exertions.

Pippa turned her head to look at her. "It certainly is up there, all right," she managed to get out between gasps, struggling to sit up to see to where she had seen Jonathon standing. There was no one there. Her heart slowed—had she seen him there at all? Or had she just conjured it up herself in all the excitement? Whatever it had been, she had *known* on some level that if she opened her eyes, he would be there, watching her. She had felt no surprise, only confirmation of something she always carried within her.

"You're great, Pippa," Fiona carried on. "It took me until this third visit to be able to join in with this dance. I always wanted to, but thought I would make a total twit out of myself. But you, you just got straight on up there."

Pippa shrugged, the chill of the night air now getting to her. "I didn't have much choice, to be honest. The guy who dragged me up there wasn't taking no for an answer."

"What guy?"

"You know, one of the leaders. I can't really describe him as they are all dressed the same. But he seemed bigger and stronger than the others."

Fiona looked at her with bemusement. "But I saw you get up! You were looking at the stars, smiling, then you looked at the dancers and virtually lurched to your feet to throw yourself into the beat!"

"Wh…what?"

"Nobody dragged you up, Pippa honey. The sea air must be getting to you. That's what I was saying, you're great to have joined straight in."

Pippa lay back on the ground, looking at the stars but not seeing them this time. What had happened? Had the alcohol been more potent than she had thought? Had Jonathon been watching her at all? Casting her mind back, she found she couldn't get a clear grasp, and what was more, she didn't really mind. It had been an amazing experience, a clashing kaleidoscope of feelings, and really, wasn't that all that counted?

*

Jonathon put out a hand over Juliet's cup to stop the waiter refilling it. Honestly, it was just like being in charge of a child. She was dressed in deeply unsuitable clothes for an evening on the beach, the filmy gauze of her purple shift affording her little protection from the elements. The strappy sandals were equally ridiculous. Yet it didn't seem to perturb her at all—instead, she seemed glad to cling onto Jonathon's arm. Perhaps that was why she had worn such high heels—it gave her a good excuse not to leave his side.

They sat at the banquet tables sheltered by the dunes, the first-class dining experience for the Princess Coral's guests having been exemplary. The only problem he had was Juliet. George and Nina had stayed aboard the ship, and Jonathon got the impression that they were looking forward to a break from their demanding, often petulant daughter. To compound matters, George had put Juliet into Jonathon's care, asking him to look after her.

Juliet aside, he had enjoyed the Maori experience but had quickly understood that the show put on for the guests and the one for the staff and the locals were two different things. As the evening wore on, he found it harder and harder to resist the drum call from the beach. When Juliet went to the bathroom, he made his escape, ensuring the Bradleys would look after her when she returned.

As his eyes adjusted to the star and firelight, only by a flare of his nostrils would anybody have known that he was taken aback by what he saw. Pippa. Hair sparkling and shining as though on fire. Her body, stretched to the stars, showing her slim belly as her top rode up. Arms outstretched to the sea, breasts high and firm, pressed against the thin silk of her shirt, then crouched to the ground, butt straining against the combat trousers she wore, riding low on her shapely hips. Then moving fluidly up to the stars again, down and around. She was part of the beat.

He willed her to open her eyes.

To feel his stare.

To connect to him, in her tribal moment.

Her eyes opened and fell directly upon his. The fire cackled, throwing her face into relief. Clearly lost in the music, her soul stretched out of her eyes and into his. The sparks hissed, bringing shadows. Jonathon stepped out of the circle of light to seek refuge in the dark.

He couldn't peel his gaze from her as she danced with renewed vigour. My God, she was simply amazing. Was she dancing like that for *him*? His body tightened involuntarily, as he wished it were simply the two of them with this beat on the beach by the fire. A groan escaped his lips as his imagination had him running his hands up her bare sides to her arms and cupping her full breasts, savouring their weight in his hands, trailing kisses up her soft neck to taste her rosebud lips, the heat of the fire allowing them to lose their clothes, the beat of the drums picking up pace as…

Rubbing his hands through his hair, he bit his lip hard to drag his thoughts back from dangerous territory. Wasn't he supposed to be controlling these thoughts? How could he, when he couldn't get her out of his head? But it couldn't lead anywhere. He ran down the list of why again. She was the head chef, he the CEO, and he was out to prove all CEOs weren't soul destroying philanderers. Thinking of Mulberry and Pippa together had the same freezing effect on his blood as a cold shower would have. He left the beach without a last look and found his way back to his insipid date.

"Oh Jon-*hic*-athon, I'm so happy you're back." Juliet teetered toward him, arms outstretched for him to catch her. Barney and Della Bradley cast an apologetic look at Jonathon before heading down to catch the Xplorer back to the ship.

"Where are the lovely Bradleys going?" Juliet slurred her words. "Come back, Darney and Bella! We were just beginning to enjoy ourselves!" There was no response from the pair as they scuttled away. "Well, they sure ain't no fun!"

"Have you chased them away?" Jonathon put the last five minutes away for safekeeping, and concentrated on being the CEO of Queen Cruises. The most important thing now was to keep happy the daughter of his most important client.

A pout appeared on Juliet's face. "I only asked whether they would be up for a threesome." Jonathon stared at her. Had he heard right? "Oh, not you too. I was only teasing dear Darney and his mouse-like wife. I would never have gone through with it. And it's had the advantage of chasing them away so we two can be alone." Juliet leaned in to kiss Jonathon, whose delayed shock reaction allowed her to land her lips on his cheek.

"Juliet, I think you have had quite enough to drink." How many times had he said this to her, and he only met her yesterday? He steered her toward the bay. The last boat of the night was due to depart in ten minutes. It had been made clear to everyone on the way out that if they missed this boat, they would have to sleep in Whangara and get the first boat out in the morning before the ship departed at six a.m. No one wanted to miss this last boat. The last vestiges of the staff were making their way there, and against his will, Jonathon felt himself searching for Pippa.

"Did you hear me, Jonashon?" Juliet looked as though her eyes were going to fall out of her head as she swayed dangerously.

"Hm?" Jonathon held her up as he looked around for Pippa, wishing he could just brush Juliet away like the irritating creature she was.

"I cantch walk 'nmore." She stumbled against him. "And I feel very shi..ick!" The last syllable was forced out of her by a retch as she stumbled to her knees and promptly returned all the hospitality she had received at Whangara, inevitably splashing Jonathon's brown Timberlands.

Great. Just great. He hunkered down beside her. "Are you all right?"

"Nooooooooooooooooooo." The wail that came back at him was nearly as strong as the stench of sick. "Do I look—*hic*—alright? I can't walk..." Her voice started to fade. "I can't even...even... get up." She lay down fully on the beach, eyes closing in a stupor. Damnation, could this night get any worse? This silly twit of a girl was in a heap at his feet. He weighed up his options, and recognised that there was only one. Bending down to her, he reached his hands under her arms.

"Come on, old girl, I'll have to carry you." Stifling a groan, he heaved her to her feet, swung his arm under her knees, and lifted her up. Staggering, he eventually found his balance and made his way with great care to the boat.

"Ooooh, Jonashon, you're the besht. I love you so." Juliet snuggled her head under his chin, and with her hand started playing with the buttons of his white cotton open neck shirt.

"Juliet, stop that right now." This was the last thing he needed. After all his thoughts about Pippa, Juliet's hand inside his shirt left him a feeling a little bit nauseous.

"Mashterful," sighed Juliet before closing her eyes and plastering a big happy smile on her face. Had she planned this to get into his arms? Perhaps he was crediting her with a few too many brain cells.

As they neared the boat, more people joined them, mainly staff. He saw a few fingers pointed, heard a few giggles and some "ahoy there Mr. Eagletons," but it was Pippa he was looking for, and he soon enough caught sight of her. She was talking to one of the Maori leaders, and his dark complexion provided the perfect contrast for her fiery colouring. As ever, she was laughing. Why did she never laugh with him? He would give anything to be that Maori leader right now, smiling down into her upturned, beautifully sweet face. To her side, he spotted Rob watching him with a dark look. He breathed deeply to help carry Juliet's dead weight and tried to think straight. Juliet snuggled closer.

"Jonathon darling," she breathed.

Of course. The answer was right here in his arms. All he had to do was give the impression that he was looking after Juliet. Obviously, he couldn't let people think he was in a relationship with a guest, but he could certainly use a deflection and Juliet, who was such an attention seeker, would provide the perfect cover. Surely then no one would believe anything of himself and Pippa. He could keep his reputation intact and maybe, just maybe, Juliet may stop him thinking of Pippa. He had no other answers for now; this would have to do.

He was just boarding the boat when he felt someone fall against him.

"Sorry, oh I am sorry."

A bolt of lightning went through him as he recognised Pippa's dulcet tones. If he was going to put a barrier up between them, he may as well start now. His heart sank to his boots at the thought, but so be it. He could never do anything with his attraction for Pippa.

"Watch where you are going, please."

Pippa looked at him with sparkling eyes, then looked at Juliet in his arms. Her green gaze clouded over. A little frown appeared on her face, before total incomprehension blanketed her features.

"But…" She stopped there, as her hand flew to her mouth. She glanced down to the floor, but not before Jonathon could see confusion, which turned her eyes luminescent. "Nothing." She muttered the word at him, turned her back, and marched on board.

Jonathon watched her go with a deep ache in his belly. His gut twisted, his heart fractured, but his mind was calm. The die was cast.

*

After the gentle light of the stars, Pippa now felt naked under the florescent lights, with the plastic seating of the boat providing no hiding place for her. She had to quell the rising desire to race back to the beach. Run away from Jonathon and the jumble of emotions shaking their way through her, each one vying with her for the most attention, like small children. Seeing a window seat free, she collapsed into it gratefully, staring unseeingly out into the dark night.

What had just happened when she was dancing? When she'd seen Jonathon, her body froze, her soul soared. Surely he must have felt *something*. The incredible feeling of looking *in* at someone—of baring her soul and allowing that someone to see in to her—rocked her to the very centre of her being, and she was damned if she could make sense of it.

And then…then! She discovers him with Juliet in his arms. The irony of the situation didn't escape her either. She had been dumped by her boss whom she thought she loved and who loved her, and had ran away from London because she didn't want to see him with the latest *it* girls. Now here she was, harbouring feelings for her CEO, who had the ultimate *it* girl in his arms.

Jeez. A girl could get a complex.

They obviously enjoyed flirting with her until it was time for them to get serious about another girl. Fine, she could handle that. Just keep a grip on her imagination, which was travelling farther and wider than her physical body, thinking Jonathon cared about her. Forget about men, focus on her career and who knows, maybe the next few days would fly past and then she wouldn't have to be in such close proximity with Jonathon.

Men schmen, who needed them.

Refusing to hear a small voice deep within her, she stared gloomily at her reflection of the window. She wouldn't fancy her either—her nose was too small, her hair a total state, her mascara never seemed to stay on...

Fiona and David, gabbling away furiously, sat down beside her. She turned from her naval gazing and smiled over at them.

"Did you see Mr. Eagleton and Juliet Stevenson?" Fiona looked at her with excitement dancing in her eyes. "How exciting! Do you think they'll get married? Will we all be invited? Will *Having It All* magazine be there to take photos? Oh, I can't believe this, it's so romantic. Wait 'til I tell my friends back home, they'll think I'm making it up!"

David laughed at her infectious chattering. "He only carried her back to the boat. She must be very drunk, judging by the look of her. And a dickie bird told me that she puked everywhere, including on Mr. Eagleton's shoes."

Fiona's peals of laughter rang through the boat. "Exchanging bodily fluids already!"

David gave her a mock frown. "Not quite exchanging, love. And no need to be crude."

Fiona leaned into Pippa's shoulder. "What's up? You've gone all quiet."

"Oh nothing, I'm fine." Pippa plastered a smile on her face. She *was* fine, really. She knew what she had to do.

"Come on, what's up? I don't know you all that long, but I do know when someone isn't happy. You looked as though you were having a whale of a time, until now." David groaned at her pun and she cast him a sideways look. "Not my best, I admit, but I am trying to get a smile here!"

Pippa chewed on her bottom lip. She had another ten days left—would she go stark raving bonkers if she didn't have someone to confide in? Calling anyone back home was hardly an option. And she trusted Fiona and David. What the hell. She leaned back in to them. "I know you're going to think I'm a complete twit, and sorry for that. But—" Fiona interrupted her.

"Hang on, I get the feeling this is about a man?"

Pippa lifted her chin with a rueful smile. "Am I so transparent?"

Both David and Fiona grinned and spoke together. "Yup."

"Great. That's all I need. Anyway, this bloke—"

Again Fiona cut in. "It's Jonathon Eagleton, isn't it?"

Pippa stared at Fiona. How on earth had she pieced that together? Was the girl psychic or what?

"You're upset at having to share with your CEO."

Pippa sat back in her seat, a wry twist in her tummy.

"Fiona, why don't *you* tell the story?" David rolled his eyes at Pippa, mouthing "sorry" at her. "Will you ever be quiet and let Pippa speak?"

"Yes, yes, sorry Pippa. Go on. I'm right though, aren't I??"

"Keep your voice down, for Pete's sake. Yes, you are. I don't know how I can share the same suite as him until the end of the cruise."

"It must be tough, all right."

Pippa smiled at her. "I can spot the sarcasm a mile away. I don't need David's help for that."

"Look," Fiona gestured apologetically, "you have no idea how good your situation is. You have your own room and en-suite—have you even seen our accommodations?"

"No."

"You should come around and check it out. We share a bathroom with three other people, and we have to queue for hours in the morning. If it weren't for the fact that you were a new, senior member of staff, people would be getting seriously pissed off at the fact that you get the preferential treatment." Fiona held a hand up to Pippa, stopping her from butting in. "I know, I know, it's not your choice, nor is it your fault, but some people could choose to see it differently. Anyway, where was I? Oh yeah, *and* you get to share the same space as the wonderful Mr. Eagleton. What could possibly be wrong with that?"

The fact that I am hopelessly attracted to the wonderful Mr. Eagleton.

Try as she might, she couldn't raise a smile. "You're right, of course you are." She gave a brisk shiver. "I'm just missing the warmth of the fire."

"Oh, wasn't it so lovely…"

Pippa sat back and listened to her friend gossip about the evening, and managed to nod in the right place. Maybe some things weren't meant to be made sense of. Like the Maori who had plucked her from the beach to dance.

Juliet's breathless giggles floated back into the large boat from the cockpit.

How *romantic*.

She could only imagine too well the lowness of the lights, casting Jonathon's face into rivulets of shadows, and Juliet making the most of the darkness. Her heart hardened. Of course Jonathon didn't fancy *her*, a lowly chef. Why would he when he had the billionaire's daughter hanging off every word he said?

She crossed her legs. Heck, she could get through this. No problem at all. It was only a matter of time and space.

She only had another ten days to get through, but precious little space to do so.

Chapter Seven

Pippa couldn't believe it when the twenty-four hour break from the ship loomed close. Ever since Whangara, she had kept her head down, learning as much as she could, and avoiding Jonathon. When they did meet, she did her best to be coolly casual to him, but couldn't ever bring her gaze to meet his, afraid of what she may see, or worse, afraid of what he might glimmer from her. Her dreams were a traitor to the cause though, for night after night, she was wakening with images, both salacious and innocuous, of the two of them together, circling, weakening her resolve.

They sailed through the vivid blues of the waterways between the two islands, and through the Queen Charlotte Fiord. Whenever Pippa could get up on deck or out on her balcony, she feasted her eyes on the unfolding landscape. The high cliffs were covered in various shades of green, broken only by white gushing waterfalls and sharp brown jagged rocks. Scudding white clouds completed the exotic look, and even as it was dangerous, it was inviting too, and her heart constricted in desire to get out there.

As they neared Kaikoura, her stomach twisted in excitement. The passengers had twenty-four hours on shore so she could do whatever she wanted to.

Coming back to her suite after breakfast service, she put on her hiking gear that she had left out the previous night. She laced up her trusty boots and a bubble of excitement rose up from her belly and came out of her mouth, singing quietly to herself. She strode over the gangway without a backward glance at the Princess Coral, watching instead the emerging landscape. The road snaked through the green hills to the National Park, beckoning her closer, and she was still humming when she signed into the book—arrival time, intentions, and what time she aimed to be back down. She bought some refreshments, and, wriggling into her daypack, headed off on the trail, breathing in deeply the rich, fresh air.

The trail led her into an ancient beech forest, with laden trees groaning overhead. The ground was smothered in brown, red, and orange leaves, which crunched beneath her boots with a satisfying crisp noise, loosening the smell of damp, loamy undergrowth. When she looked upwards, the azure blue of the sky was such a direct contrast to the reds and browns of the early autumn trees that she nearly succumbed to the desire to fling herself backwards onto a bed of leaves and gaze up through the vivid hues. Later, on her way back down, then she would have plenty of time but for now, her aim was to get up to Surveyor's Peak, see the view and get back down before dark. She may love hiking, but hiking on an unknown trail in the dark was a minimum of fun, especially one that was teeming with wildlife but devoid of humans.

Several hours later, she climbed, panting and gasping, to the peak. Her reward laid itself out before her like a patchwork quilt when she reached the top: the ship, a toy boat nestled in the bay. And if she peered hard enough, she could see the coast of the north island. She forgot to breathe as her eyes drank in the view, not being able to get enough of it.

Taking her camera out of the case, she clicked shot after shot of each direction. Thankfully, there was no one else there to disturb her peace and quiet, although someone special to encase her in a bear hug whilst they looked at the view together was a thought she had to push aside.

Even her sandwiches tasted better than they should've done out here in the bright, crisp air, but once she had demolished them, the hike back down started calling out to her. She took one last look, then, feeling like a bit of a twit, she threw her arms open in the direction of the sea and let her head fall back so she could see the sky. She concentrated on expanding her diaphragm from her stomach up, drawing oxygen up through her lungs, and expelling with a quick force. It was a relaxing action until time encroached upon her. Shaking her head, she glanced to the south only to see dark clouds gathering. She quickly packed her backpack and it was then she saw him.

Jonathon.

Ruggedly handsome, he was dressed in dark jeans, hiking boots, and a burnt orange jacket. The upturned collar just grazed his square, lightly stubbled jaw, and his hair was delightfully messy. Just looking at him made her yearn to run her fingers through it. The burnt orange of his jacket heightened the dark colours of his eyes, yet she could've sworn light emblazoned from them. Her stomach twisted, and her legs yearned to carry her to him. Who was she kidding, thinking she could deny the attraction she felt for him?

It assailed her.

But how long had he been standing there? Had he seen her display? She glanced at him to see a smile curve his lips. Yup, it looked like he sure had. Boy oh boy, she felt like a prize idiot now. She put a hand to her mouth to suppress the giggle that was starting deep in her belly, feeling a little intoxicated from the deep breathing Jonathon had just borne witness to. As she thought about it from his viewpoint, the giggle escaped in a whoosh and she lowered her eyes, which were flooding with giggling tears.

"H...hi," she just about managed to get out.

He put his head to the side, and eyed her up and down, and she felt each touch of his gaze as though he physically stroked her. "Do you know what I think, Ms. Renshaw?" Jonathon's voice was dry, the sound of a smile breaking through.

Not trusting herself to get one more syllable out, Pippa just shook her head.

"I think you are a little bit mad, and a little bit funny, and a little bit serious..." He started walking the short distance between them. "And a little bit cute, and a little bit quirky, but most of all..." He stopped in front of her. "A little bit kissable." With that, he took her hand away from her mouth and dropped a quick kiss into the palm.

A squawk escaped from Pippa as in one smooth motion, he took her into his arms. Her heart sped up to beat uncontrollably and she stared, mesmerized, as he bent his head to press his lips against hers. Her lips felt so sensitive under his warm, hard kiss, which took the remaining breath out of her along with a soft *oh*. They came alive—they were parched and Jonathon an oasis.

When the gentle tip of his tongue reached out to outline her lips, a bolt of electricity shone through her, setting her senses on overload. She pulled back to stare up at him in shock, her fingers aching to reach out to touch his face, to entwine themselves in his hair. His dark head was outlined against the bright sky, and she wanted nothing more than to scatter her thoughts to the wind before saying, "Yo, you big stud, take me to bed or lose me forever."

But quotes from *Top Gun* were not remotely helpful. Deciding not to say anything rather than gabble like a goose, she stood out of his electrically charged space. Chest rising and falling rapidly, she waited for him to speak, her legs doing a reasonably good job of holding her up, despite having turned to jelly.

He ran his hands over his face and put his fingers back through his hair—*but I want to do that*—and took a shaky breath. "Look, Pippa." He spread his hands out toward her. "I don't know what happened there. I'm sorry, it was unforgivable for me to behave like that toward you. I just couldn't resist." His mouth twisted in a rueful grin, which slowly died as his eyes met Pippa's.

Pippa tried to think straight, but it was hard with desire nipping at her. Why had he kissed her? More to the point, why apologise? He must regret it already. Whereas she had loved it. She had never been kissed so...so...*masterfully* before. And God, look what it had woken within her. How was she going to beat her attraction now? She should join Attractions Anonymous. *Hi, my name is Pippa Renshaw and I am inexorably attracted to a man who doesn't feel the same way.*

He stared at her, an unreadable look on his face.

"It was unforgivable, actually, you're right." She forced herself to talk to him, anything to try to stop her awareness of him, of his full lips and his quirky smile and his *hot* body... dammit. "I don't know what you thought you were doing. I mean, you are the CEO and all that. You should know better!" Lack of oxygen brought her rant to a halt just in time for an ominous rumble. The dark clouds rolled and multiplied by the second, and clashed into each other, cymbals in the sky.

"Come on." Jonathon reached out to her as though to grab her by the arm but stopped just short of touching her. "We need to find shelter—if that storm hits us out here, we'll be in trouble." He turned and strode off, and Pippa trotted behind him.

"Are we heading for the trees? We'll get some shelter there, at least." She was puffing as she spoke, pulling her hood out from under her backpack.

"No, there's a tramping hut here, tucked out of sight. I stayed there a few years ago. Quickly."

A fat raindrop hit the ground beside Pippa, and another one to the front of her. The heavens opened, the loud *shush* of the downpour drowning out all other sound. Her visibility narrowed as sheets of grey water slanted to the ground, and she focused on Jonathon's orange jacket ahead of her. Winds gusted around her, buffeting her sideways, and the weight of her backpack doubled as the water seeped through it. Rain laid siege to her from all angles, bouncing off the hard ground.

"Here." Jonathon had to shout to make himself heard, and he reached out to grab her hand. "Stay with me." He slowed his pace to hers, a solid anchor for her to cling to.

*

Jonathon held Pippa's cold hand, resisting the urge to tuck it into his pocket. That would be too personal. Mind you, after that kiss, what was too personal? He didn't know what had overcome him—all he knew was that when he saw Pippa standing there, outlined against the cerulean sky, arms flung outward, that he had to kiss her.

No other thoughts had entered after that one.

He put his head down against the wind and angled his upper body so his shoulder sheltered Pippa at least a little bit. The air turned biting cold, but he radiated warmth throughout, knowing she was by his side. He couldn't forget the way her lips had moulded to his, the way she'd turned delightfully pliable, and his lower stomach tightened imagining just how soft she could be. Given half a chance, he'd love to find out, but he had to draw the line at a kiss. Pippa had been wide-eyed and beautiful as she pulled back, but she had been right. That was where it stopped.

It only took five minutes to reach the hut, but it may as well have been a lifetime. Pippa stood on the porch shivering, her legs and backpack drenched, but a wry smile wreathed her face. Jonathon opened the door, and they tumbled into the shelter of the hut, dripping on the stone floor.

"How lovely!" Pippa sounded surprised.

"Have you been in a trampers' hut before?" Jonathon unzipped his dripping jacket to leave it hanging on the porch, and stretched his hand out for Pippa's jacket to do the same. She took hers off, looking around with a smile.

"Never. I expected it to be more of a—oh, I don't know—a basic shed. This is luxury, in comparison. Look, a kitchen and everything."

The hut was an L-shaped room, a kitchen of sorts tucked away in the corner with hanging pots and pans, a large wooden table, and chairs. A huge fireplace was set deep in the stone wall, with sleeping mats against the opposite wall.

"New Zealand is well set up for tramping. It makes a lot of money from tourists from all around the world coming here. They know how to do it right, make sure they come back again." As Jonathon spoke, he wondered whether they would be making use of the sleeping mats. The rain hadn't lessened, if anything, it seemed to be worse. Night was only a couple of hours away.

Pippa shivered as though the same thought crossed her mind.

"So get your wet gear off before you freeze. There should be blankets somewhere—go have a look while I light the fire." Jonathon crouched by the fireplace, checking out the cast iron box beside it. Just as he'd thought, there was plenty of fuel and the fire laid. He lit a match to the kindling, appreciating the sound of the dry wood taking to the flame.

Pippa came over, holding her boots and socks.

"That was fast!" She hung her socks by the fire and placed her boots as close as she could to the flames.

"The huts are well looked after. Whoever is the last to leave lays the fire ready for the next trampers. With a bit of luck, the fire will be blazing soon so we can dry our clothes in order to head out again. Speaking of which, you need to get changed." He looked at her to see her apprehension, freckles standing out against her pale face. She didn't move. What was the problem? Getting undressed with him around?

He blew gently on the kindling to avoid the emotions that soared through him at the thought of Pippa dressed only in a blanket. Fine, there were no drums, and they were far away from a beach, but they had the fire and they were alone. He hauled his thoughts back and looked at Pippa to see her looking thoroughly miserable.

"Pippa, you'll catch your death of cold, so go around the corner and take your clothes off. There should be a cupboard with some dry blankets. Find it, get a blanket, and get out of those clothes."

"Sir, yes, sir!" She turned and padded around the corner before he could trust himself to look back at her.

"So how do you know so much about these huts?" Her voice travelled back to him as he undid his boots with ice-cold fingers.

"I've been in this part of the world for nearly two years now. I've just moved to New Zealand, was living in Melbourne until now. I spent a few months hiking around when I first came out to this side of the world and ever since, I've wanted to move here." He took off his socks and shook them outside, water dripping from them.

"So you like hiking?" Pippa's voice sounded muffled, as though her head was in a cupboard.

"Yup, anything outdoors really, hiking, kayaking, climbing, you name it, I love it. That's why New Zealand is perfect for me, gives me many opportunities to get out in the wild. My job keeps me busy and it's nice to know that any spare time I get, I can be straight out there. No wasted time. Like today." He paused and looked at the rapidly building fire. Much as he loved getting out, the older he got, the more he wanted someone to share the outdoors with. Someone to watch the stunning scenery with, to work through a tough hike to reap the rewards, to turn and look at her and smile as if to say, "Hey babe, we made it." To be in a trampers' hut on their own, a bit like…this.

The thought rocked him.

"How about family, do you not miss them?"

Jonathon lost himself in his thoughts. Did he want to commit to someone? Was it his age? Or was it because it was Pippa?

"You don't have to answer." Pippa's voice became louder as she appeared, shuffling around the corner, looking for all the world like a western Geisha Girl, yet with a heavy blanket restricting her movements. She had tied the blanket like a toga, over one shoulder to leave the other one bare and there were a few freckles on that shoulder just begging to be kissed. He had never known something as shapeless as a blanket could form such alluring attire, but it skimmed over her slender figure, falling in neat folds to the floor. One of the folds crept open as Pippa moved closer to the fire, providing him with a glimpse of a long, slender calf. His throat went dry as he watched her peg her clothes out to dry, taking care to hide her bra and knickers behind her t-shirt.

He looked up at her, flummoxed as his mind took the blanket from her to expose her creamy flesh. When she paused in her shuffling to look at him questioningly, he broke his thoughts off with an internal flick of his head.

"Sorry, what did you ask?"

"About your family, do you not miss them?" She sat on the chair furthest from him, crossing her ankles neatly together to close her knees, reminding him of the day in the Stevenson Hotel. On one hand, it seemed like yesterday and on the other it felt as though he had known her all his life. Hadn't she *always* been with him?

"Oh, my dad died when I was twelve, left me and my mum in a lot of debt." He sat back on his hunkers, then thought better of it as his bare heels met his sodden jeans. He stood instead, not meeting Pippa's gaze, sure he would find only sympathy there.

She said nothing. Smart girl.

He carried on talking, strangely uplifted by telling her. "As soon as I could, I left school to work. When Dad died, we had to sell the house but the debt was bottomless. Mum held down three jobs at the minimum wage just to ensure I had warm boots on my feet. So the day I left school, I vowed to myself I would buy her a nice house where she could put her feet up and buy all the boots she wanted. Three years later, I did." He stopped, remembering the semi-detached house he had bought her—or them, as he had still lived with her then.

Pippa's voice broke into his memories. "Penny for them." Her voice was gentle. His eyes lit on hers, and a warm feeling made its way up from his belly to emerge as a smile.

"Just thinking about the house." His voice came out gruff, and he cleared it. "We moved from a fifth storey flat into a semi-detached house, and I painted the outside pale yellow. It was Mum's favourite colour. She loved it, and never stopped telling me so. I guess it was my first proper home." He glanced sideways at her, seeing her in the soft light, her face smooth in relaxation with a quirky lift to one side of her mouth.

She tilted her head to the side, and looked upwards at him, her eyes turquoise in the firelight. "Well done. You'll be buying her a primrose private jet soon."

"No way. I love hiking, climbing even, but hey, don't get me in the air in only a tin can. I can't do it."

"What do you mean?" she watched his lips as he spoke and he had to look away from her bright gaze.

"I can't fly." He laughed, a bright sound that took him by surprise. "Well obviously I can, otherwise I wouldn't be on the other side of the world to where I grew up. I hardly sailed here. No, I mean I hate flying. Brings me out in a cold sweat every time. Long-haul flights are the easiest to cope with, being as there's a stretch of time between take-off and landing, so I can attempt to relax. But short flights? Hell no. You wouldn't catch me dead on one."

Pippa bent her head to look at him lopsided. "I guess we all have stuff to deal with."

The words sounded dreamily husky to him and he caught her clear, honest gaze in her upturned face, glowing in the light of the fire. She smiled at him, and he could see her genuine interest in him and what he was saying.

He cleared his throat, trying to clear the salacious thoughts that were coming hot and fast.

"Are there more blankets?" He had to get away before he did something silly. He walked around the corner, smiling to see a dark blue blanket folded neatly on the kitchen table for him.

His jacket had withstood most of the wet, so his t-shirt was dry enough to leave on. But so much for waterproof trousers—they still had a way to come before they were as efficient as the jackets.

As he came around the corner, having stripped off from the waist down and wrapped a blanket around him, Jonathon paused to watch Pippa. A faint blush from the fire graced her cheeks, and her rosebud mouth shone red. Perfectly formed ringlets corkscrewed around her face, with curls alternating between a burnished bronze colour and a glowing amber. He couldn't drag his eyes away, just wanted this moment to last forever. Something outside the window warranted her undivided attention, as her white teeth were busy chewing on her lower lip, and even from her profile, he saw she wore a small frown.

He gave a little cough, afraid that if he looked at her unawares for much longer, there would be no hiding his reaction to her. The fire crackled like a machine gun as his less than noble thoughts started charging the atmosphere.

Pippa jumped, and turned to look at him fully. She was flushed and couldn't quite bring her eyes up to meet his—they lingered instead on the blanket wrapped around his waist. "What, did your top not get wet?"

Jonathon almost laughed as he took in the accusatory look on her face. "No, sorry about that." His voice was as dry as his t-shirt. "I guess my rain jacket provides better coverage than yours, *Little Miss Independent, I love hiking on my own!*" He crouched down to attend to the fire, and settled in a chair beside it.

Pippa smiled a crooked smile. "I guess I asked for that. I have no excuse for being caught out in a storm with poor clothes and no backup plan. Sin sin." Jonathon raised an eyebrow at her. "It's Irish, don't ask me to explain, I can't. It means that's that, like, c'est la vie, or...or...oh, I don't know and stop looking at me like that!" She pulled her blanket closer around her, blowing a curl away from her face.

"I didn't know you had Irish blood in you." Jonathon felt his heart grow bigger as he looked her. She clearly felt the need to talk when she was nervous. A bit like an Energizer bunny, just give her something to talk about, an edgy situation, and she was off.

Her words kept coming, and he switched off from them, not because he wasn't interested, but because shifting emotions changed her face when she talked, which fascinated him. There was a melodic lilt to her voice that he hadn't noticed before and he very nearly started swaying in time to it.

A note of flat sarcasm entered the melody, and he blinked. Pippa stood and if the blanket would have allowed it, he felt sure her hands would be on her hips. What would happen to the blanket then? He gave an inward groan at the path his thoughts had taken, and hauled them back. "What was that?"

"I said my granny was a mud wrestler, and you smiled and said how nice."

Jonathon felt his face start trembling in an effort to keep it straight. "I'm sorry, I was listening."

"Sure." If her voice had sounded musical before, it now sounded like a b-flat. "What time is it? I think it's time we left; the clothes must be nearly dry." She shuffled over to the fire to take down her still wet clothes.

"Pippa." Jonathon tried to intervene. "Even if the clothes were dry, the weather isn't going to let us out of here anytime soon."

"I'm sure it's manageable." She shook her trousers out firmly, and winced as a loud slap came from the sodden legs snapping against each other. Her blanket started slipping from the knot she had tied over one shoulder, and she grabbed it back up impatiently. Eschewing her knickers, she tried to force one long leg into the wet trousers.

Watching her and her attempts to keep her modesty intact, Jonathon felt like a heel. "Pippa," he tried again, and going over to her, put a hand out to help her balance.

"I'm fine." Indignation came off her in waves. "I just want to get out of here, sooner rather than later. I don't want to be making a bigger fool of myself, twittering on about stuff!" Her pronunciation was crisp and clear. How could he tell her he hadn't quite listened, preferring rather to watch the light play on her lovely face?

"Right, great, I'll even help if I can. I'm just asking you to come with me to the door to look outside. Please." He stretched a hand out to her. Pippa gave a final, useless yank on her trousers, then dropped them. The gesture allowed her blanket to swing open, and Jonathon caught a glimpse of her waist, which curved out into her hip and down into her upper thigh. Her skin looked so soft, smooth, and peachy. Jonathon felt a long awaited throb of desire shoot through him as images of him running his hands over her body besieged him.

She pulled the blanket closely around her and, squaring her chin, stood tall and ignored his hand. "I'll come and have a look, dry my clothes, and get out of here."

"Okay, okay," Jonathon murmured, hoping to quell his desire.

Pippa's shoulders slumped as she gazed out at the rain that was coming down in sheets.

"Maybe it will clear up soon." She muttered the words through a cross mouth.

"Why don't I call down to the office and let them know we're here. I'll ask for the forecast too." Jonathon didn't know what to think as he unlocked his phone. They should go back down as soon as possible. His hopes weren't quite on that wavelength, though, for the time he was spending here with Pippa made him happy. She made him happy, with all her strops and gabbling and reactions—and, let's face it, she was damn sexy, even in that blanket. Jonathon took a deep breath. It was thoughts like these that were going to get him into trouble one of these fine, or indeed miserable, days.

"Sure, yes, I understand." He disconnected the call and turned to face Pippa. "Bad news, I'm afraid. The storm is set to last until the early hours of the morning, so the recommendation is to stay here for the night. They did tell me to root around in the cupboards, where we should find some store food and drink, so at least we'll be fed and watered."

Pippa hopped from one leg to another. "Oh well, that's just marvellous." There was a pause. "First things first, I need the loo. Where's the long drop, do you know?"

"Oh, the joys at being out in the wilderness!" Jonathon stopped short as Pippa's scowl deepened at his jocular tone. "Just around the corner. Here, put on my jacket, it'll keep you drier than yours will. There are plenty of blankets so you can just swap when you get back."

He held his jacket up for her to slip her arms into. "I can put it on myself, thanks." Pippa took his jacket and managed to wriggle into it without exposing any more bare skin, and slid her bare feet into her sopping boots. "Urgh! If there's one thing I don't like about the rain, it's putting on wet boots. It puts me in a thoroughly bad mood." She looked at him with one eyebrow raised and it was clear she thought she was issuing a warning.

"In the meantime, I'll have a look and see what stores we've got."

Pippa turned and clumped off, his jacket nearly overwhelming her, but, at the same time, provided her with enough coverage for her to move more freely.

Jonathon started whistling as he looked around the hut with greater interest now that they would be staying the night. Not wanting to question too deeply the cause for his good mood, he distracted himself by finding the store cupboard.

The Kiwis certainly knew how to do things. He found dried pasta, sun-dried tomatoes, and tins of tuna, along with cans of peas and carrots. To top it all off, there was a nearly full bottle of

Milford Whisky, New Zealand's finest. This was fantastic. There was just no way this would be found on the hiking trails in the UK.

He decided to leave the cooking to the professional, and instead found two glasses and poured each of them a generous measure. They needed warming up internally, as well as externally. Since he was assiduously banishing thoughts of how he and Pippa could warm up together, the whisky would just have to do.

*

Pippa stood on the porch of the hut, shivering despite the comfort of Jonathon's coat, looking into the sky for any sign of relief from the driving rain. She turned the collar up and buried her face into the soft inner fleece. Jonathon's smell contrived to warm too, the smell of sea pines, needles being crunched underfoot to release their sweet but spicy smell. Inhaling deeply, she closed her eyes and allowed herself just one thought of how wonderful it would be if it were Jonathon's arms wrapped around her.

And here she was, about to spend the night in a confined space with him. How was she going to manage to keep her hands to herself? She had a secret smile to herself, for she had seen him look when her blanket had opened, and knew exactly what was on his mind when he'd tried to help her into his jacket: her blanket would have gaped open for him. There was no doubt he was interested in her as a woman, but would he be interested in any woman he was bound to spend the night with? What was she thinking?

He's your boss. Forgeddaboudit. You made that mistake once, which took up four years of your life. Do not do it again!

Her resolve stiffened, she opened the door and tried not to let the wind take it off the hinges. She finally managed to get it closed and hurried over to the fire to sit and take her wet boots off. She held her cold toes up to the fire and Jonathon came up behind her, putting a glass with amber liquid under her nose. She took a sniff. Turning around to him, she smiled. "I don't believe it! Whisky?"

"I know, the Kiwis know how to do things. There's nearly an entire bottle, I assume it's here for medicinal purposes. Here." He handed her the glass. "This is yours, drink up. There's also plenty of food for when we get hungry." He grinned at her, his blue eyes mirroring his smile, and held his own glass up to clink hers.

Unable to resist smiling back, she clinked his. "Cheers."

Pippa was silent, savouring the taste of whisky in her mouth. She wasn't much of a whisky drinker, preferring a less obvious taste, and if she did drink shorts, it would normally be gin or vodka. However, neither gin nor vodka provided the same warming glow as the whisky slid down the back of her throat and trailed fire as it made its way into her stomach. Her face started to heat up, but pleasantly.

"Much as I like seeing you in my jacket, you're looking a bit warm."

Yeah, mister, warm I can deal with, but not you checking me out dressed just in a blanket. The warmth of the whisky continued down to her lower belly and pooled there, causing a lot of delicious sensations. Her toes wiggled all by themselves.

"I'm fine, thanks for your concern." She knew she should move away from the fire, away from the heat of Jonathon's gaze, away from this crazy situation. "I should check out the food, I'm starting to get hungry. What do you fancy, what is there to cook? I hope we can manage something nice. That would be good, wouldn't it?"

Pippa walked backwards from him to escape around the corner. She put her hands up to her face and cupped it, running her palms into her eye sockets.

Nerves suddenly hit her like a ton of bricks.

A premature night was closing in.

Here she was, in the wilds of New Zealand.

Nobody was around for miles.

Except her CEO. The one man who, she was finding out fast, could evoke intense desire in her with just a raised eyebrow. And all she had to wear was a blanket.

Oh. My. Word.

Chapter Eight

Pippa looked through the food Jonathon had left out on the wooden table. The sun-dried tomatoes would need soaking for a while, but with them she could manage to put something not half bad together. The concentration needed helped her to ignore their situation. Draining the cans of vegetables, she found a knife and started to chop, hoping that she wouldn't chop off her fingers because her hands shook so much.

"So what do you think?" Jonathon called from beside the fire.

"Not bad, I think we can eat fairly well. Give me an hour and we'll see what it all tastes like."

An hour. She had an hour to calm down, and cooking always helped her peace of mind. Humming slightly hysterically to herself, she flew around the makeshift kitchen. There was olive oil too, great. She was going to be proud of this meal.

"Now, if I could have a newspaper to read," said Jonathon, "that would really be the icing on the cake."

"Don't push your luck!" she retorted back, but smiled at the domestic scene. Domestic? What was she thinking? This was *wild!* She was getting hot in the outdoors jacket. "How're the clothes drying? I need to take your jacket off but would prefer to put on my clothes rather than be encumbered with this blanket." She was standing at the gas camping stove. There was a pause, then she heard him get up and his shirt appeared in front of her.

"But what are—" She swung around to him and stopped, eyes widening. Jonathon stood there without his shirt, just a blanket wrapped around his waist. She stared at his broad shoulders, his clavicles sharply outlined, and his firm chest, pectorals clearly defined. His arms were to die for—there wasn't a pick on them that shouldn't be there. His shoulders tapered down to a slim waist, and his six-pack in between just begged out for her hands to run over it.

She swallowed. What could she say now? She couldn't meet his eyes for he would see desire stark on her face. Desire to press a kiss in the hollow of his neck, to step into his arms and to let her hands roam over his torso. A flush was starting to work its way up from the curling of her toes.

"Put it on, I don't mind." His voice came from a distance. "That smells really good, Pippa. I have to say if you're going to get stuck out in the wilderness, preferably do it with an accomplished chef."

Pippa stared up at him, only hearing *do it*.

He smiled. "I didn't quite mean it like that, or maybe it was a Freudian slip. You go and change, and I'll plate it up."

Pippa mutely nodded, and escaped to the relative coolness of the fire. Shrugging off the jacket, she put his top on to discover it came down to her knees. And bonus, her knickers were dry. What the hell, she was sick of dragging the blanket around with her anyway. Stepping out of it, she felt fresh and cool for the first time tonight, and yes, okay, sexy.

Jonathon came around the corner. "Here you go." Handing her plate over, he stopped and whistled, the look on his face one of frank admiration. Her rationale told her she was wearing something but she still had to glance down to check.

"My shirt has never looked that good on me."

Pippa nodded again, wanting to say, "Oh, but it has." This time she managed to bring her gaze up to his. "Dinner. Whilst it's still hot. Let's eat." Great, she went from a nodding pony to a stilted parrot.

"Have another shot of whisky, keep you nice and warm."

Closing her mind to the thought that he may be trying to get her tipsy, she nodded and threw her shot straight back.

This time she wasn't arguing—she needed all the Dutch courage she could get.

*

"It was a great supper, thank you." Jonathon raised his glass to her.

"Would you like anymore? There should be some in the pan keeping hot, I hope it did. Keep hot, I mean. Would you like some? I've had plenty. Or we could pack it up for tomorrow or leave it here for the next hikers, mind you, it may go off and start smelling before someone else is here. So perhaps it's best to eat it now, would you like some? I won't be offended if you don't want any more, honest." Could she ramble anymore?

"I'd love some, you must be a mind reader." Jonathon handed up his plate to her, the look in his eyes warming her face. She didn't need to be a mind reader to know exactly what was going on behind that dark amber gaze. The colour turned molten as she looked down at him, or was it liquid bronze? It was fascinating the way his eyes kept changing shades from dark whisky to amber and other times, the gold flecks dominating his pupil. She stood, biting her bottom lip in concentration. So what colour were they really?

He arched an eyebrow. "Everything to your satisfaction, Ms. Renshaw?" The words were low and sounded hard to say, as though they had been forced out.

"Pardon?" Pippa shook her head in confusion. "Sorry. Yup. More food. Did you want some?" She grabbed his plate without waiting for an answer and walked to the kitchen, feeling his eyes roaming up and down her back. What was she like? She had to get a grip. Stop talking for one, have another drink, then go to bed.

*

Jonathon sat up and poked the fire, causing a log to crash and sparks to fly busily up the chimney. He was enjoying the sight of Pippa in his t-shirt. She must have had no idea of how sheer the material actually was, but at least she had her knickers on. He didn't think he would be able to control himself if she was totally naked underneath. It was hard enough trying to keep his eyes off her breasts, the nipples straining against the shirt, bouncing slightly every time she moved.

He had enough to eat, hell, she had given him enough to feed a horse, but he wanted her only to be relaxed and confident. And it also gave him an opportunity to watch her walk around.

Win-win.

She padded back to him, and handed him a plate full of food. "No more for you then?"

"No, I've had enough." She hadn't—Jonathon had watched her pick around her food.

Pippa ignored her chair to sit cross-legged by the side of the fire, and pulled the t-shirt down. Her slim back outlined against the shirt, she gazed intently into the depths of the fire as though just by looking deeply the fire would divulge secrets never before told.

He picked up the whisky to pour a shot into her glass. Pippa smiled her thanks, then cradled it against her breasts. He was doing his best to give justice to her food, but all he really wanted was to be that glass. He sat up abruptly to hide his stirring desire.

"Did you always want to be a chef?"

She smiled into the fire and he saw the confidence surge back to her in the straightening of her spine. Tilting her head to the side, she looked at him from under lowered lashes.

"I did, yeah. I'm very lucky in that my mum introduced me to cooking at an early age, spotted I had talent, and nurtured it. I've always known I wanted to work to create new recipes that give people pleasure when they eat."

Miles away, her eyes turned spearmint green in obviously pleasant recall. She smiled at him, held her tumbler up as though to congratulate him, and returned her gaze to the fire.

Jonathon enjoyed the smooth silence that had fallen, but he missed the sound of her voice. "Any other dreams need fulfilling?"

Pippa smiled and dropped her head down and shook it from side to side, allowing her curls to bounce haphazardly. "Well..." She threw him a teasing glance from below her eyelashes. "You'll just laugh."

Jonathon felt a smile start deep within his belly, and all his consciousness zoomed in upon her. Nobody, heck, *nothing* existed outside their little hut.

"Try me." He sat back in his chair, stretching his arms up and crossed them behind his head. "I'm all ears."

"I've always wanted to swim with dolphins." Pippa pursed her lips in a wry smile. "Do you think that's silly? A bit, oh, I don't know, hippie-ish?"

"No, why would I? It's lovely to have things to aim for, and why not swimming with dolphins?"

"It's just I love swimming, especially in the ocean, and think how amazing it would be to have dolphins sharing your water." She stopped and stared back into the fire. "They're special, dolphins, happy creatures and I think they wouldn't share their water with you unless they *chose* to do so. Which would make *me* feel very special. I couldn't imagine it." She leaned her head on her knees and turned her green gaze on him. She was miles away, her face softened into a gentle look. He could see how she must have looked when she was a child, sweet, innocent and with her whole life ahead of her.

A blink, and she was back in the room and looking at the fire. He wanted to be close to her.

He wanted her to look at *him* closely, wanted to be able to see the changing colours of her eyes up close. See if he could track them. What would happen if he ran his fingers up her arm, for example? Would they turn forest green or a lighter shade?

"That's a lovely thing to aim for. How about now? Are you searching out the secrets of the universe?" Jonathon's voice was low and husky, and without being fully aware of his actions, he dropped down to lie beside her. Supporting his head on bended arm, he angled himself in order to be able to look as deeply into her face as she was the fire.

Pippa glanced at him quickly, but it was enough time for him to see the desire and confusion causing her pupils to dilate.

"It's a secret, don't you know." Her voice shook.

"Well…" Jonathon reached out a hand and pulled on a curl, watched it bounce back into place. She looked at him and watched his lips, entrancing him. "I think…" Jonathon shifted closer, then sat up fluidly. Her eyes grew heavy and she looked hypnotised. "It's all about pure…" he took her face in his hands, "physical," his lips descended on hers in a feather like kiss and he breathed the final word on the corner of her mouth, "attraction."

His heart was beating uncontrollably, and for a brief second he was afraid it might come right out of his chest. The tantalising kiss he had dropped on her warm lips had only served to bring him teetering on the knife-edge of wanting to drag her into his arms and he trembled in the effort of pulling back a fraction to see her reaction.

Her eyes were half closed and she swayed toward him as he pulled away, putting her lovely, dishevelled head to one side, offering her lips to his. With a groan, he wrapped his arms around her and pulled her close.

In a quick movement, his t-shirt was over her head and her near nakedness enflamed his wanting to where it very nearly hurt. His mouth descended on hers, a hungry kiss that demanded satisfaction, and he ran his hand through her hair, up and down her back, delighting in the feel of her. She felt so much better than in his wildest dreams. The yearning that coursed through him was molten lava, pure primal passion where his mind cast off rationale and embraced desire.

With a wrench, he stopped, a guttural moan escaping him at the effort, and looked fully at Pippa. "Are you sure?"

Her eyes fluttered open and her lovely, opaque gaze told him everything he needed to know. She nodded and murmured softly, "Yo, you big stud, take me to bed or lose me forever."

Jonathon put his head back and gave a roar of laughter before he slowly drew her long legs alongside his and allowed the tide of desire to take him.

*

Pippa stretched and yawned, a slumberous cat. Her limbs were heavy, and her body felt so happy her lips just would not stop smiling. She kissed the hollow under Jonathon's clavicle, flicking her tongue out. He groaned and her insides fluttered at the sound.

"I was nearly asleep."

"Mmm, me too, only I'm *starving*."

"No wonder, you ate nothing."

"Yeah, I wonder why, with you looking at me as though you were about to devour me!"

"Go get some food then, but quickly, I want you right back here where you belong."

Getting up lithely, Pippa made to put some clothes on, but Jonathon grabbed them from her. "No way, lady, I'm not done with you tonight."

Pouting provocatively over her shoulder, Pippa said, "But I may be done with you!" and walked out of sight into the kitchen. She returned with his still-laden plate and, sitting on her hunkers in front of the fire, finished it off quickly so she could return to Jonathon's warmth.

The whisky bottle was still half full, so she poured a glassful, then taking a small sip and holding it in her mouth, leaned across to kiss Jonathon. When they came up for air, Jonathon expelled a long breath. "You have no idea what you do to me."

"Show me then."

*

Lying there, satiated, listening to Jonathon's deep breathing, Pippa nearly pinched herself. What had just happened between them? She'd had sex before, of course, but never with such a spell-binding connection. All she wanted was for her body to dissolve so she could melt into him. When she'd thought she was completely aroused, Jonathon took her up a level, and yet another until she mewled and shook with the intensity of the orgasms that wracked through her, creating a buzz from the top of her head to the tingle between her toes.

Jonathon stirred beside her, half awakening. "You know," he murmured so quietly that Pippa had to wriggle up closer to his lips, "I think we'll have to find some dolphins sometime soon."

Pippa lay there, hand on his chest. She smiled against his neck and hugged him tight.

A cold thought of the future at work came knocking, but Pippa turned it away firmly.

Mustn't think about anything. Just sleep.

*

A shaft of early sunlight fell across Pippa's sleeping face and Jonathon felt an urge to kiss her smooth skin. His watch told him it was five a.m. and he sat up slowly and gently, extricating himself to put on his clothes, and went outside onto the porch. It was a calm, beautiful morning, the kind that follows a storm—but he couldn't appreciate the wonderful meadows that surrounded the hut.

All he could see was trouble ahead. What was he going to say to her when she woke? It had been an amazing night and he was shaken by the depth of his feelings for Pippa. Through this enforced night together, he now knew her on so many different levels. Going forward, how would he resist her?

But what choice did he have? He was in the middle of difficult negotiations with the Stevensons, and should they come to an agreement, the publicity was going to be huge. He could not let it be known that he, CEO of Queen Cruises was shacked up with his head chef, whom he had only just met. His name would be mud. If only the timing was different, if only he had met Pippa elsewhere. Mulberry's face appeared before him, smirking.

The crew, like any new crew, waited for him to make a slip up, ready to pounce. As it was, they no doubt were suspicious of his and Pippa's accommodation. He ran his fingers through his hair and looked to the brilliant blue sky for inspiration. Despair slumped his shoulders. He didn't want to hurt Pippa. How was he going to explain himself to her? He should've braved the damn storm and gone back down to the ship. Instead, he had made the most of being with a woman who intrigued him, and look what had happened.

A noise from inside sent a tremor through him. She was awake. Pushing the door open, he stood there to watch her stretch languorously and had to quell the desire to go to her. Damn, this was hard.

"Hi." He averted his eyes as he came in, hoping to divert his thoughts. "How did you sleep?"

"Great—but what are you doing out there? Are you not coming—"

He felt her gaze on him as she stumbled to a stop and inwardly cringed for the havoc about to be wreaked.

"Pippa."

The pink tinge in her cheeks turned to a sheet of cold at the tone of his voice and she struggled to get up whilst covering herself. "Oh, Jonathon, don't worry—it's clear you want to forget what happened last night. Well good news for you, so do I. Let's clean up and then walk the hell out of here." Her normally soft face was all edges and angles as she pushed her hair back from her forehead and gave him a hard look. She grabbed her clothes and scrambled around to the little kitchen and soon the sounds of clattering and ferocious banging came to him.

Closing the door behind him, he went in to help. Her back was to him, and her shoulder blades were hunched together, her head on a rigid neck. It spoke volumes to him. Putting a hand on her upper arm, he tried to pull her around to face him. "Look, Pippa—"

She shrugged her arm from his hand, stepping away, then glanced quickly at him. "Please, let's wait until we're outside." The look in her eyes called to mind a winter's ocean, and he felt the deep cold wash through him.

It only took five minutes—the kitchen was tidy and Jonathon cleaned out the fire and re-laid another. Lucky sods who were going to be here next. He heard muttering from Pippa.

"Sorry, what did you say?"

"Nothing you'd want to hear. Are we ready? Good, let's go." She stalked past him, her head high.

*

Pippa's heart weighed at least a ton. Who knew such a small organ had the capacity to feel so heavy? The moment she'd seen his face, excitement had replaced her previous anxiety over where he had disappeared to—until he'd spoken. Regret had filled that one word, and if that weren't enough, it was written all over his face.

Flinging her backpack on, she gulped in the welcoming fresh air. She was such a twit sometimes. She had promised herself she wouldn't do this and what had she done at the first opportunity? Leap into bed with him. She didn't understand. What she had felt when leaving Marcus was nothing compared to this level of devastation. Jonathon had peeled a layer from her soul, laying her bare, vulnerable. Damn. She should never have let this happen.

She should've left in the storm last night—getting lost and even suffering from pneumonia would be nothing compared to this.

She felt his hand on her shoulder, and looked at it through a haze of confusion.

"Pippa, wait. Please listen."

Okay. Let's give him some time. Her newly battered heart gave an extra beat. Perhaps it would be okay. She nodded.

"I had a wonderful time last night." His voice was soft, and he put his hands, his large strong hands, on her shoulders and pivoted her to face him. Dare she hope? His craggy face was downcast, tawny eyes asking her to listen, and she heard the soft rasp as he ran his hand over his chin.

"It's just that…" He trailed off, and a shard of despair hardened her. He was gazing out to sea. "It's just that—"

She shucked off his touch. "No need to explain. You're the boss, I'm only the chef."

At her words, he swung to her, eyes blazing. "You're not 'only' anything. You're a fantastic chef, the best there is."

"But not good enough for you." A cold mirth rose in her to escape in a barking laugh. "I should've known this would happen. I was fool enough to think you might care. Whereas you were just being the boss and being all power hungry, thinking you could get anything you wanted." Her voice started to rise. She stopped and took a deep breath. She was scared of the depths of sadness waiting to embrace her and hugged her anger all the more closer to her.

"I mean, the clues were all there, I didn't pay heed to them." Her blood started to thin, to race around her, shepherding heated thoughts through her. Blast him for not wanting her. "Ever since we met, you have been making snide remarks about girls sleeping their way to the top. No doubt you were biding your time, sure that I would fall into your bed." She breathed out through pursed lips.

Calm down, it's okay, you can get through this too.

"No, I wasn't, Pippa, I promise you. Please listen to me. You're the kind of girl I could fall in love with…" He stretched a hand out to her, tawny eyes a deep velvet brown with hope. Seeing how his hair fell over his forehead was nearly her undoing.

"Here comes the 'but.'"

"Listen to me, please. The reason I made that jibe about sleeping with your employers was because I had been informed that Mulberry hired girls who slept with him. I guess…" He glanced at her stony face but received no encouragement and shrugged, a bitter smile on his face. "The idea was fresh in my mind." He massaged his fingers through his hair as though washing out the idea, his lips flattened into a long line.

Pippa blinked. She gave a slight shake of her head. What was he saying? He had thought she had slept with Mulberry to get her job? She started nodding, and couldn't stop.

"You thought I slept with that sleaze bag Mulberry to get my job? And so you thought, being the new CEO, that I'd sleep with you too?" She held a hand out to stop him from answering. "You thought I'd be easy pickings, hey." Her stomach rolled, sending up deep-wracking sobs. "And it turns out I was. I don't believe I fell for it."

She turned to escape the intensity of his look, wanting to be on her own.

She was betrayed.

Chapter Nine

Jonathon watched her retreat through the forest. She kept pulling up the straps of her backpack and he could tell she was irritated at having her stride interrupted. She squared her shoulders and soon disappeared from view.

He found a boulder to rest against and checked his phone for important messages. There were none that required him to return to the Coral Princess liner directly, so he sat still, looking up into the clear azure sky. What on earth kind of a pickle had he gotten himself into? He had not only slept with a member of staff, albeit a senior member, but he had inadvertently paid her the greatest insult that he could imagine paying a woman. No wonder she had reacted so forcefully. What had made him say it? Was he questioning her integrity? Did he just want to hear her deny it? Or was he putting the final nail in the coffin of their relationship? Whatever it was, it had certainly brought about a hasty end to it, platonic or otherwise.

More to the point, how did he now feel about the fact that Pippa had not slept with Mulberry? If he were being honest with himself, he had started to doubt it soon after the dinner she had cooked for the Stevensons. Not only did she possess talent, by the bucketful, but she had integrity and something deeper, soul. No denying her innocence after today. There was a certain sense of relief that she had denied it so vociferously—he couldn't have contemplated a future with her if she had done it with Mulberry. He hauled his thoughts up short. A future? Was he now thinking of a future with her? She was wonderful, true, but did he want her to feature in his future?

Who was he kidding, of course he did.

The thought of waking up beside her every morning, seeing her head on the pillow beside him, warmed him from within.

Hot on the heels of this realisation came the multitude of accompanying problems.

He couldn't have a relationship with her, a member of staff. That was a fact. There was a tentative trust amongst the staff for him, this news would rekindle the same low morale that he had been working so hard to eradicate. He couldn't compromise his hard work or his good name. Could they get away with having a relationship in private? He shook his head irritably. Of course they couldn't, that was a recipe for disaster. Plus, he had too much respect for her to ask her to do that. What was he going to do, dammit anyway.

Out of his peripheral vision, he espied some chamois coming to graze in the nearby meadows. Slowly moving his head so as not to alert them to his presence, he looked at them fully. It was a funny animal, neither goat nor buffalo, but rather a cross between the two that was found only in New Zealand.

The meadow it moved in was simply breath-taking, banks of thigh high wild flowers streaming to the west in the wind, a riot of yellows, blues, pinks, violets with tall strong grass breaking them up. The dense green background of the forest provided the perfect foil of dark shadowy shapes to the bright gyrating dance of the flowers.

He didn't know what to do. Unless he wanted to propose to her right now to show everybody he wasn't like Mulberry, he couldn't have a relationship with a member of staff. And as much as he liked Pippa, proposing was too daunting a prospect to consider.

He would just have to get over her. He would just have to shut his heart to her. He could do that. Couldn't he?

*

Pippa boarded the ship, breathing a sigh of relief that she had made it back without Jonathon catching up with her. Not wanting anyone to see her—with swollen eyes, bedraggled hair—nor to pick up on the air of sadness she was sure she carried like a mantle around her shoulders, she hurried to her suite.

It smelt of him, and the tears that she had been holding back since seeing the ship now threatened to overwhelm her. From the moment she had looked up to see him standing darkly in the doorway, backlit by bright sunlight, her stomach had twisted with the knowledge that she had made a fool of herself. What really hurt was the fact that he had given the impression he was interested in more. Had he deliberately gone out of the way to hurt her? Was he laughing at her now, or thinking he'd give her a few days to cool off then try his luck again as she was so damn gullible?

And had he known about her affair with Marcus Longbottom? She had imagined so, came to the wrong conclusion from his oh-so-knowing looks, which she knew now to have been about Mulberry. He didn't know about Marcus. Her heart sank even further. Should he ever find out, no doubt he would think her hypocritical in her reaction. What a mess.

Don't think about it. Just get on with your day.

Jean-Pierre was leaving the ship that day, and she wanted to have a last talk with him. A small thrill ran through her at the thought of being solely in charge of her first kitchen, but it was dampened by her mind playing tricks on her. As she had felt the excitement, for a fraction of a second, her mind had assumed it was because of Jonathon and she had felt happiness pierce her like a ray of sunshine through the gloom—only to have the darkness descend fully as she realised anew what an arse she had made of herself.

Here she was thinking about him again. To work.

It was only when she reached the kitchens, that her tightly held jaw unclenched and she embraced the distraction work provided. Fiona appeared, complete with clipboard.

"Hey, Pippa, did you have a nice hike? You look…" She paused whilst she looked at Pippa with sharp eyes. "Different, I guess."

The desire to open up and get some sympathy from Fiona nearly threatened to overwhelm Pippa. As it was, her eyes filled with tears at the mere thought of a hug from her.

"It was fine. I'll talk to you later, if I may." Blinking away the tears, she looked at Fiona properly. "So what did you all do? Did you have a good night?" *Distract me, please.*

"Yeah, it was great, we just ended up in the nearest pubs. And you know the Kiwis, only too happy to welcome strangers. Actually, the night turned into an impromptu leaving do for Jean-Pierre. Which brings me along to the reason I'm here—we're holding a proper do for him in Akaroa. Are you coming?"

"I'll come straight after service." A thought struck her. "If he's leaving, does that mean there's a spare bed in staff accommodation?"

"It does, but it's in the men's quarters. Don't tell me you want to swap your life of luxury for one of squalor?" Fiona started laughing but stopped when she saw Pippa looking grim. "Aw, what's up honey?"

"I'll tell you later, I'll be a wreck if I go into it now. Except for one thing—I need to be out of that suite. I don't care where I sleep, it could be anywhere except there."

"You can't sleep in with the men though." Fiona glanced away, unseeing. "But I'll tell you what. As David and I are senior members of staff, we have a twin away from the bigger staff rooms. We sleep in two singles pushed together. I'll ask him to move in to Jean-Pierre's place and you can share with me."

"You'd be a life saver, Fiona, are you sure?"

"Course I am, David won't mind at all either. It'll do us good to have some space for a change. We don't have an en-suite though, so be prepared for queues!"

"I'd even love queues, the mood I'm in at the moment. Can I move in today between shifts?"

"Absolutely! Great, I'm going to get lots of glossy magazines when we're on shore, and we can spend hours sitting up and gossiping. I'm really looking forward to it."

"Thanks so much." Pippa leaned over and hugged her friend. "I'll see you about four, in your place."

"Our place!" Fiona winked at her and carried on to advertise the leaving to the rest of the staff.

Jean-Pierre came over to her and put his arm around her shoulders. "Bonjour, Peepa. You are excited, non?"

"Oui, Jean-Pierre, very much so, and a little bit nervous too."

"Non non non, you are not to worry, you are a *vraiment* good chef, and the Coral restaurant will be busier than ever it 'as been."

"Thanks, Jean-Pierre, I'll miss you."

"One thing I 'ave to remind you about is the Gala Dinner on the last night. You will 'ave a full restaurant, all two hundred seats 'ave been booked. I don't need to tell you this, but I will anyway. The waiting staff can be slow, so you need to be at the service counter *all* the time, making sure all five courses are taken out on time. So whatever you are overseeing will all 'ave to be done by five p.m. as the customers seat at five-thirty."

"Thanks for the tip." Pippa didn't want to examine her feelings about the dinner, for she was sure she would uncover a mass of nerves wriggling around like worms. Five courses for two hundred people was one thousand plates of food. Yikes.

"All the ordering has been done, and the fresh supplies arrive on the morning. Now, 'ave you any questions?"

"Non, merci! Only, can I have your mobile number in case things go drastically wrong and I need help?" Pippa was laughing but she was semi-serious.

Jean-Pierre gave a sigh, and flung his arms out theatrically. "Only now as I'm leaving does my petit chou ask for my number. Oh my 'eart, 'e is broken."

Pippa nudged him. "Oh, get on with you! Don't make me

laugh—it's well known that you are leaving here to set up a French vineyard with your lover, so don't come all coy with me."

Jean-Pierre smiled at her, eyes softening with concern. "And if you need a job, you come work with me, you could run the restaurant. It 'as a Michelin star, you would be perfect." Jean-Pierre paused to kiss his bunched fingers. "And I could concentrate on the wine!" He clapped his hands in delight. "What a team we would make! 'ere is my number." He handed it to her and pulled her toward him as she stretched her hand out to take it. "Forgive me, Peepa, you don't look 'appy. I 'ope everything is bon, but if no, come and work with me again!" Holding her by the shoulders, he kissed her resoundingly on both cheeks. "Now, we must work, but I will see you at the drinks tonight."

Pippa watched him go with mixed feelings. She was sad he was going, but happy at the chance it provided. It was lovely for him to offer her a job, but he wasn't serious, surely. She would love to spend a couple of years exploring New Zealand, rather than cruise around the coast line, watching as trails she wanted to hike were taken away from her.

*

When lunch service was over, Pippa picked up a large empty box to put her belongings in and headed back to the Doubtful. *Dear God, please don't let him be there, please. Let me just get my things and go.*

She had knocked on the door and had turned the handle before the sound of giggling came to her. Her insides twisted themselves in a knot and sent a large volume of blood to her head. Of all the worst scenarios she had pictured in her head, Jonathon having Juliet in the suite hadn't even featured as it was too horrible to imagine. Normally Pippa loved her chef's whites, as they spoke of professionalism to her, but now she looked in dismay down at them. They weren't a pristine white after the busy service, her hair had escaped its ponytail, and she may as well not have put any makeup on this morning.

Dreading what she was going to see, she leaned against the door to open it. They were standing by the balcony, Juliet clutching a wine glass by the stem, and Jonathon holding a coffee cup. Her heart jumped, stalled, then bunny hopped into an uneven rhythm. She couldn't look at him—afraid her misery would make itself all the clearer if they made eye contact.

Glancing at Juliet hardly helped either. If Pippa looked a fright, then Juliet looked a cool, perfect vision in a lemon shift that skimmed over her barely there breasts and fell to just above her knees. *I should be with him, not you!* The thought was gone even before she could acknowledge it.

A voice from the balcony indicated that George Stevenson was out there, talking on the phone. She must have interrupted a business meeting. At least she had knocked!

"Pippa." Jonathon nodded to her, his face devoid of expression.

"Oh yes, you." It seemed as though Juliet had rammed rods of steel through her words. "We didn't order room service, did we? Or maybe we ordered champagne?" Juliet put one hand on Jonathon's torso, the other around his back, clearly very possessive. "I'd like some sparkling water as well please, room temperature with a slice of lemon. Only one slice." Juliet raised one eyebrow at Pippa as though to ask her why she was still here.

Pippa felt a snarl rise up through her, and she caught it and struggled to hold it in. To have to put up with this after last night's charade was making her mad.

"I think you must be confusing me with somebody else. At the moment, I'm the person who's moving out of this suite."

Juliet looked slowly at her, blinking her eyes in a way that reminded Pippa of a snake. Then a slow curve appeared on her face, masquerading as a smile. "Well then, don't let us delay you."

Juliet turned her back to Pippa, clearly dismissing her. Did she care? Like hell.

With her bedroom door safely shut between them, Pippa sank to her knees. Jonathon had looked shocked, but what did he expect? She couldn't stay there with him. She resisted the temptation to throw herself on the bed crying and ran the water for a shower instead. This may well be the last decent shower she would get for a while.

*

She listened at the door, and didn't pick up any noises to indicate they were still there, so heart thumping, she gently opened it. "Oh!" The exclamation came out before she could stop it. Anthony, one of the porters, was sitting on the sofa, leafing through the company brochure.

"Hi, Pippa. Mr. Eagleton called down to us and asked one of us to help you move your stuff."

"Th-thanks." Pippa didn't know what to say but fortunately Anthony was oblivious to her bemusement. Jonathon's thoughtfulness had taken her by surprise. She could manage all her things, but it would be a struggle. How considerate of him to ask Anthony. He must have been thinking how to help…

See, here she was softening toward him again. *Stop that!* Before she would know it, she would have herself convinced that he really had liked her, and must have had a good reason to treat her the way he had. Rather than a bastard who had taken advantage of her, and then flung the fact that she had succumbed to his charm right back in her face, along with one of the biggest insults she ever had received. Not quite the biggest, Marcus was lucky enough to hold that trophy, but close. Her professional self-confidence was on the wane again. Perhaps she was no better than the men she slept with.

"This is lovely, ain't it? I'll betcha loved staying here." Anthony's cockney accent stoked her homesickness, which had laid in abeyance until now. She was turning into a mess. "Is this it then, love?"

"Yes, thanks, Anthony."

He hoisted the box on his capable shoulders and stepped back. "After you then." Thankfully, he chattered away, distracting Pippa whilst she locked up the Doubtful.

Ha! No better name for the home of Jonathon Eagleton. She would be damned if she ever crossed that threshold again.

Chapter Ten

Jonathon rumpled his hair and sat back in his chair, breathing slowly. His office always had been small but now it made him feel claustrophobic. There was no room for him to get up and pace.

Despite all his efforts, the Stevensons were no closer to signing the contract. It would be such a coup for both him and Queen Cruises, he couldn't give up on it. Queen Cruises was floundering, thanks to Mulberry. The company desperately needed the cash injections that would come from a partnership with the Stevensons. Not to mention the positive publicity.

Their meeting earlier on had been cut short, as George's phone call had resulted in him having to attend an online conference. They were due to resume in the Doubtful in ten minutes.

Peering into the small mirror he had by the door, he straightened his tie and pulled tall his shoulders. He wasn't going to accept no for an answer, at least not without a bloody good reason. The Coral Princess kitchen was buzzing as he walked through it, preparing for dinner service.

"Mr. Eagleton?" Rob came up behind him, walking fast to keep up with his pace.

"Yes, Rob?"

"We're having a leaving party for Jean-Pierre tonight in Akarao, at the Old Tiger's Head on the quayside, starting about nine."

"Great, if I'm free I'll come along for a drink."

I wonder, will Pippa be there? He dismissed the errant thought, but it led to wanting to see her. "Have you seen Pippa? I need to talk to her about some canapés for the Doubtful." What was he doing?

"She's just going over the restaurant bookings with Christian. But I've got the canapés ready to bring out now. Would you like to check them?"

"No, it's okay." Disappointment shot through him like a shard of crystal glass. "I'm sure they're great. Thanks, Rob."

Walking to his suite, he took several deep breaths. Forget about Pippa, at least for the next hour or so. Find out what Stevenson needed in order to convince him to do business with them. Concentrate on pushing this deal through.

It was obvious George Stevenson was in a bad mood as soon as Rob opened the door to him.

"George, how are you?" Jonathon said.

"Not great, Jonathon, I warn you. Juliet wanted to come along, but I need to explain some things to you without her being here. She didn't like it when I said no. But some things are better left to the men, hey, Jonathon?" George raised the whisky that Rob had given him and threw the entire contents back. "Thanks." He winced as he swallowed and handed the glass back to Rob. "Black coffee, please, young man."

This was going to be harder than expected. Damn Juliet anyway. What had she said to rile her old man, and why had she chosen this evening to do so?

"Come out to the balcony. Rob has set some canapés out there, and some more drinks." Jonathon held an arm up to take George outside. Perhaps the fresh air and the dusky view would help to relax them both.

"Heck, it sure is nice being out here." George looked out at lights coming on in the quayside. "So, Juliet has an idea, one she's not letting go of."

Jonathon smiled at George. "Oh?"

"I'll be straight with you, Jonathon. I promised her, before we decided to come aboard with you, that she could take a more active role within the Stevenson Corporation. She has decided, in her wisdom, to be the person within the corporation to deal with Queen Cruises. She has been privy to all my thoughts regarding our deal."

Jonathon wanted to shake his head in disbelief. Surely George hadn't agreed to this preposterous idea? No wonder Juliet had kept tagging along with her dad.

"Juliet wants me to sign the deal with you, but in return," and here he held up a warning finger, "she wants you to take her on to the board of executives, as PR executive."

Jonathon ducked his head, thoughts cycling through his mind but no answers becoming apparent.

"Oh, and something else she wants…" George paused, and turned away from Jonathon to lean over the balcony rail. "Fire Pippa Renshaw. I don't know why but she seems to have taken a disliking toward her."

Shock jolted through him. Had he heard right or had he just *thought* George had voiced aloud the ever present name in his head? Mad though it sounded, he had a sneaking suspicion that his ears hadn't failed him.

"Let's clarify, George." Waiting until he got the nod from Stevenson, he continued. "You and I will sign the deal, and we send out a PR statement saying that Stevensons Hotels and Queen Cruises are going into partnership. In return, I fire one of my best chefs—no, make that my best chef—and also take Juliet onto the board of executives?"

George looked at him, the lines on his face becoming more prominent. "I'm afraid so, only the deal will be co-signed by both Juliet and myself."

Deep breath. He would find a compromise.

"May I ask you something, George?"

The older man nodded.

"What experience does Juliet have?"

George shrugged. "Not much, as you know. But the kid has to start somewhere, and although her name will be on the deal, she won't be able to do much without my say so. We can make sure of that in the fine print, if that will put your mind at rest."

Jonathon's adrenaline started pumping. There had to be an answer here somewhere. He didn't know which was worse, holding his best chef—*Pippa*—to ransom, or having to put up with Juliet ad infinitum. Dammit, he was counting the days already until he could get away from her.

"Any PR experience at all?"

"Juliet is exceptionally good at courting the paparazzi and, Jonathon, to be honest, I think that she will be extremely good in a PR role. I know Queen Cruises is without a PR executive, as she left with Mulberry."

"Yes, but Juliet as an executive?"

"Like I say, she won't be able to do much on her own. On the plus side, she already has her own PR machine in place, and they really are all exemplary. I don't see this as a bad thing for either my corporation or Queen Cruises. We would be putting a lot of money into this deal, and I wouldn't jeopardise that."

Jonathon said nothing. *Let George keep talking and see what's on offer.*

"In fact, were we to sign the deal, she would ensure an explosion of publicity. She has been working on it already, and I like most of her ideas. I wouldn't demand you put her on the board unless I thought she was up to the challenge."

Jonathon took a beef Wellington canapé and chewed on it. So it was a demand, was it?

"Obviously, even though she is a Stevenson, I would expect her not to be treated any differently. She would, as I've told her, submit to your decisions as final."

But she's pulled the wool over your eyes. Of course, you think she's capable of making it a success, she's your daughter.

George fell silent, but there was a tick in his jaw as he watched Jonathon.

"So talk to me about Pippa. That's the chef you want me to fire."

George now swung to face him, leaning his back against the railing. "Heck if I know, Jonathon. Do they know each other well?"

"No, of course they don't. How would they?" A thought struck him.

"When did Juliet tell you she wanted Pippa fired?"

"Quite early on in the cruise, after the dinner she cooked for us."

So she had been planning this ever since that first night. No wonder she had looked so smug when Pippa told her she was moving out. She was probably thinking that the suite wasn't the only place she'd leave.

"So give me her reasons to sack Pippa."

George held his hands out to him. "I'm not convinced she has any."

Jonathon raised an eyebrow. *Go easy, this is his daughter you're talking about.* The daughter of the man of the moment.

"That's the deal on the table? Either I fire Pippa and take Juliet on board, or we have no deal?"

George nodded, his eyes watching Jonathon carefully.

"Then it's no deal. Sorry, George, but I refuse to fire my best chef. Even if there was a good reason, I won't be told what to do."

*

Warmth spilled out from the pub where Jean-Pierre's leaving do was in full swing, lifting his mood. Only at the last minute had he decided to attend, and then simply because he wanted to see Pippa. Perhaps she may silence the ever-present conversation between him and George in his head. He had been none too pleased when Jonathon had turned down the deal.

He had tried to assure him it wasn't personal but he knew he had failed. For he did think it was personal, Juliet had made it so.

How dare she flaunt her status as daughter of the man with one of the greatest hotel empires in the world and demand she fire Pippa? George had said he would do his darnedest to change her mind, or at least uncover a good reason as to why she'd made her demand. Jonathon knew no such answer would be forthcoming, for Juliet was unlikely to show how mean-spirited she was by admitting to her jealousy.

Jonathon's main worry lay in the fact that he knew the Juliet always got what she wanted. Well, not this time.

Jean-Pierre was holding court to a group of avid listeners as he described the vineyard he had bought and the Michelin starred restaurant that complemented it. Soon there were cries of "take us with you!"

Jonathon smiled over their heads at Jean-Pierre, miming the action for a drink, and when Jean-Pierre shook his head, went to the bar himself. He was leaning against it, sipping his Milford whisky, when the door opened to admit Pippa and Rob.

At first glance, his initial thought was that they made a handsome couple. Pippa's dark green woolen coat was turned up at the collar against the cold, and her hair glowed rusty red against the green. He caught a glimpse of a slim thigh leading into a knee high brown suede boot. She was a refreshing sight for his tired eyes, and he smiled over at her.

Then his mind did a double take and dismay obliterated his previous—delusional, he could see that now—image of an evening spent talking to Pippa. What was she doing with *him*? He hadn't realised how much he'd been looking forward to seeing her tonight. Now here she was, on another man's arm and looking pretty enamoured at that, clutching Rob's arm and gazing up into his face with adoration. Perhaps he should tell her that he was exchanging a successful future for Queen Cruises, along with his good name, all for her job. See what she thought about him then. Although, Jonathon knew inside that she'd just walk from the job.

He could almost hear her saying, "Don't do me any favours!"

It was too late for Jonathon to escape the small bar, so he tightened his jaw and raised a hand to them. "Pippa, Rob. What can I get you to drink?"

Pippa flicked her gaze quickly into his face, not reaching his eyes. "Hello, Mr. Eagleton. We're fine, thanks."

"I insist." Jonathon nodded at the bartender for service. "Rob?"

"Milford Whisky, please. Pippa has been telling me what a wonderful drink it is."

"Really? So one for you, Pippa, as well?" Jonathon kept his face from smiling when he heard that Pippa had been saying "wonderful" in conjunction to a night with him.

Pippa's gaze met his, and the look in her eyes brought to mind a wintry day. "Not for me. The problem with Milford Whisky is that over exposure can leave you feeling quite ill."

"Oh, I don't know. It only makes me feel very good, and leaves me wanting more." Jonathon curled his hand around his tumbler, holding it warm.

"As long as there's more available, then I guess I'd have to say lucky you. It's when you run out and you have no choice but to sober up that the real trouble starts."

Rob looked from one to the other with a confused expression on his face. "Have I got this wrong, are you both whisky aficionados or something?"

"Something," agreed Pippa and she leant in to the bartender who was patiently waiting for her order. "Diet Coke for me please—surprise me with the amount of ice and lemon. I like an exciting life, me."

Whilst Rob looked even more confused, Jonathon raised his glass to his lips to hide the smile that was threatening. How could it be that even when she was mad at him, she still made him smile? Hot on the heels of this was a thought that struck him in the pit of his stomach like a hot brick, he couldn't let her get away.

*

Pippa was crying. Grief wracked through her insides, and her outward appearance struggled not to show the tremendous emotions coursing through her. Glancing through the window of the bar as they arrived, she had seen Jonathon looking very handsome in an open-necked white shirt as he sat there sipping his drink, deep in thought.

Senses she had shoved to one side now fizzed alive, sending prickles of excitement through her blood and streaming to every inch of her body. She hadn't allowed herself to wonder whether he'd be there or not tonight. Happiness flooded through her, only to be followed by a sensation of her heart being plunged into ice-cold water. Breathless, she acknowledged that, pragmatically, it would be better if he weren't here. The quickest way to get over him was by avoiding him.

Failing that, let Jonathon think she was totally over him, and onto a new man. Coquetry? Ha, Madonna could learn something from her tonight.

But why had she been so bloody minded as to order a darn Diet Coke? She needed a drink to calm her nerves. Turning to Rob, she gestured in a head movement toward the party. After he placed a proprietary hand under her elbow, she raised her glass in mocking thanks to Jonathon, and let Rob shepherd her over to the party. Why couldn't she fall for Rob? Life would be much easier if she could.

The reason sat cold within her.

Because you've fallen for your boss again, you fool.

"Peepa, Rob, welcome." Jean-Pierre waved them over to him, and pushed a glass of wine under her nose. Great, alcohol. Hopefully, her stomach would start to unknot now. "As you are at my party now, you must start trying of the wine that we shall make. And please, I want you to meet Darrel, my partner in business." Darrel was a kiwi of around fifty, a very handsome man, with a craggy face and grey-flecked thick dark hair, dressed very smartly in a dark suit.

"It is my pleasure." He took Pippa's hand and bent over it, giving it a kiss. "Jean-Pierre has been telling me all about your wonderful abilities."

"Aw, I'm sure he has been exaggerating."

"Of course he wasn't, Pippa is a fantastic chef. Please to meet you, Darrel." Rob shook his hand and looked proudly at Pippa.

Pippa's toes squirmed in her boots, and she risked a glance at Jonathon, to see a deep frown overshadowing his eyes. God help her, it was *him* she wanted to make proud—it didn't matter what anyone else thought.

"Jean-Pierre does not exaggerate. I hope we will see you soon at our little vineyard, you would be more than welcome."

"Thanks, Darrel. Who knows…" Pippa took a big drink of her chilled Sauvignon. "This is excellent!"

"Thank you, my dear." Darrel smiled at her. "Now, Jean-Pierre, you must introduce me to Jonathon Eagleton. He could be a very important contact. If we set it up right, we could get the customers from the ships coming to the vineyard. If you'll excuse us, Pippa, Rob."

"Pippa! Hooray, you're here." Fiona came over to them, dragging a laughing David by the arm. "And Rob too!" Turning her shoulder to Rob, she put her head on one side and raised her eyes dramatically at him, then back to Pippa, her question clear. Pippa rolled her eyes back.

"Great, the party's just begun." Fiona started jigging on the spot to the beat coming from the band warming up and wiggled her bottom against Pippa. "Come on, shake that booty!"

Oh what the hell! She was sick of moping anyway, and it certainly wasn't helping her to put Jonathon from her mind. Perhaps dancing would.

Chapter Eleven

Pippa's nerves melted away in favour of the thrill she felt at working her own kitchen. For the next couple of days, she was everywhere, talking to all the staff, and each time she was greeted with "chef" her heart threatened to double its size in pride. Her professional life was well on track, and for that, she was glad.

When she woke up on the second morning of being head chef, the sweet feeling of happiness surrounded her. *I am happy here, finally.* Her mind still slumbered until, with a jolt ricocheting through her, she realised her dreams had been full of Jonathon. In vivid detail, images of her as mother to two pretty girls and wife to a happy, relaxed Jonathon cycled through her head. Groaning, she sat up to swing her legs over the side of her bed and put her head in her hands, massaging her forehead as though to delete her dreams.

Fiona came in after her shower. "Headache?"

"No, just bad dreams," Pippa muttered. "*Very* bad dreams."

"Well, I'd be quick to wash them away if I were you, there's no queue for the shower."

"Great, thanks, Fiona."

As she stood under the steaming water, of its own accord her mind went back to her one and only night with Jonathon. How could she have gotten it so wrong? She had been so sure of their mutual attraction.

She blew hard into the jet, seeing if she could blow the water off course. It ignored her to continue on its way. *Yeah, I could no more switch off my feelings for Jonathon than I could divert the flow of water back up the pipe.*

Déjà vu moved smugly into her veins. She hadn't listened to herself, right at the very start when she had realised that Jonathon

Eagleton heralded nothing but trouble. But had she had a choice? She yearned to see him, yet ran when she did. Since Jean-Pierre's leaving do, she only caught glimpses of him, striding from one meeting to the next looking very stressed. Her heart ached when she saw him like that and she wanted nothing more than to be able to bake him up a batch of cookies, or give him a face massage to work away those lines.

She washed her hair vigorously. It was thoughts like these that would get her into trouble. He was an arse, he had treated her appallingly. *Hang on to those thoughts and lose the soft ones, you daft bint!*

*

"Rob?" Jonathon called out as he walked through the kitchen on his way to the Doubtful.

"Yes, sir?" Rob found him and walked with him.

"I have a meeting in the suite with the Stevensons in an hour, and I need refreshments. All the refreshments we can throw at them. Freshly percolated coffee, tea, both decaf and fully caffeinated, water, both sparkling and still, some room temperature, some chilled, lemon slices, ice, and a selection of the best pastries you can find. Plus, some fresh fruit salad and a selection of fruit as well. Oh and make sure the bar is fully stocked. I think that should cover it, unless you can think of anything else?"

Rob ran down the list with a pen, frowning as he thought. "That's it, I think, except for post coffee mints."

"Great. I'll see you there in just under an hour. I'll want to have the meeting in the dining room too, so will you make sure room service lays it out in boardroom style? Thanks, Rob."

Rob hastened off, and Jonathon let himself into the Doubtful. It still didn't feel right to him. It hadn't ever since Pippa had moved out. *Pull yourself together, man!* They had only stayed seven nights on the boat and one night up in the hut. That was *not* long enough to induce such nostalgia. Perhaps, instead, his negative feelings were the direct result of the heavy feeling of guilt in his heart.

But whatever happened with the Stevensons, Pippa would remain head chef. They could go to hell before he would agree to firing her. There was absolutely no way on earth he would ruin her professional life. Hopefully this time, Stevenson would be on his own again this time.

His hope soon turned sour when Juliet arrived, alone. Okay— he could deal with her better on her own without her adoring father.

"Hi, Jonathon, sweetie." Juliet drawled out the endearment, and planted a lipsticked kiss on both his cheeks. Struggling not to wipe the marks away, Jonathon nodded coolly at her.

"What can Rob get you to drink?"

"Well, to start with, can I have a skinny cappuccino, please? I assume you've got champagne on ice to celebrate with later."

Assume all you want, love. You know what they say about assumptions.

Jonathon looked to Rob, unsure they could make cappuccinos, but Rob was busy working to bring about what she had requested. Good man, Rob. Except for when the girl of Jonathon's dreams was on his arm. Tightening his jaw, Jonathon went over to get the drink for Juliet.

"Black coffee for me, Rob, thanks."

Sitting down on the sofa, crossing one slim leg gracefully over the other, Juliet curved her lips at him. With a start, Jonathon realised she was nervous. *Good, I can use that to my benefit.* "Let's move into the dining room, we'll be more comfortable there. When can we expect your dad?" He knew he had put Juliet at a disadvantage, and he put a hand out to help her up.

"Well, let's see. He wanted us to talk, you know, business like, and then he'll come in to see what has been agreed upon."

"So we are going to agree on something?"

"Honey-pie, I sure hope so." Her Texan drawl was more obvious now, making it clear that she was ill at ease.

He took his time settling himself at the head of the table, and waited until she had tripped around in her silly little heels to sit herself down before giving Rob the nod to serve the coffee and pastries.

"Pastries, ew, how fattening. Now, if I were on the board, I'd ensure there was a supply of non-fat goodies to eat."

Jonathon said nothing, but looked at Rob in time to see the look of askance cross his face. "Rob, I believe we have some fruit? Could you bring some in please?" Rob nodded at him and left the room.

Juliet launched straight in.

"Now, Daddy told me he had discussed you taking me onto the board of executives…"

The door opened to admit Rob.

"Juliet, if you would care to choose some fruit?" Jonathon butted in. He struggled to bite his tongue and speak at the same time. Did she want it to be known all around the ship that they were in negotiations about her being on the board? He glanced searchingly at Rob and was less than pleased to see an inscrutable look on his face. Past experience told him the more inscrutable a look, the more had been overheard.

"Thanks, Rob, that will be all." He gave the man a nod as Juliet carefully picked a mandarin from the bowl and started playing with it. Thank God she hadn't chosen a banana. The thought very nearly pushed him over the edge into laughter.

He waited until the door was shut firmly behind Rob. "Now, Juliet, you were saying?"

Juliet looked up at him and suddenly looked very young, younger than her twenty-nine years. Remorse surfaced in him, but he shoved it aside ruthlessly—this was the girl who had demanded he fire Pippa. Even if he didn't feel for Pippa the way he did, it was a disgraceful demand to make.

Juliet put a black painted nail into her mandarin and started taking the skin off. "Um, Daddy told me he had spoken to you about me being on the board of executives, as PR exec."

Jonathon nodded, keeping his eyes trained on hers.

"So I guess I was wondering what you thought about that." She started shredding the peel, not touching the flesh. Boy, would Freud have a field day.

"I want to know what makes you think you would be a good PR person." Metaphorically, Jonathon climbed aboard his soapbox and looked down on Juliet. He had to dissuade her from making mad demands and by hell, he was going to use every trick he had learned on his way to becoming CEO by thirty-seven.

"Well," Juliet perked up, "I have the plans here to ensure that the last night on board is a PR dream. Do you want to look at them?"

"No, why don't you tell me?"

"Great, well I have Marcus Longbottom lined up to fly over here to oversee the dinner. You know him, don't you? He's London's top chef, and is rapidly becoming a celebrity chef. I spoke to him—"

"You spoke to him already?"

Juliet turned fiery red. "I know him, I've been out with him a few times in London and I just kind of—"

"Just kind of what? Just kind of asked him to come over here and help out? Tell me something, Juliet." Jonathon's tone was one he deployed in order to make people want to run away and hide. "Did you ask him on behalf of Queen Cruises, or—and I'm hoping this is more the truth—did you ask him to come over to dangle on your arm?"

"Em."

Jonathon sat back and blew out a long breath of air. "Spill. Tell me your exact words."

"I, em, kind of asked him to come over to help with the overseeing, and yeah okay, to bring some publicity with him. He was thrilled, though, Jonathon, really thrilled to be asked. His agent has arranged for the BBC TV crew to come over with him. The publicity will be amazing."

Juliet wittered on, saying something about fireworks further out to sea and cocktails out on deck by the hot tubs but Jonathon's anger had reached his ears and shut off the sound.

"That was extremely unprofessional of you." He reigned in his anger to speak quietly.

Juliet flinched. "I thought you'd be glad of it all. Daddy said you needed some positive publicity, and here is a fantastic way of courting it."

"Just tell me please. Did you ask his agent on behalf of Queen Cruises, or on your own personal behalf?"

"On behalf of Queen Cruises." The mandarin peel could now join a jar of marmalade with no shame whatsoever, it was shredded so perfectly. Juliet refused to look Jonathon in the eye.

He stood abruptly, shoving the chair behind him and walked to the door of the balcony, hoping the fresh air would cool his thoughts. "Dammit, Juliet, can you see what you've done? You're holding me over a barrel. If I say no, as I want to, as I so very want to, the negative publicity resulting from this could nearly wipe out Queen Cruises." *And you want to be our PR exec.* Fortunately he managed to hold that thought in. He did need the deal signed, after all. Between a rock and a hard place, that was where he currently resided.

The sound of a sharp rap on the outside door came through, and Rob popped his head around the door. "Mr. Stevenson is here." Great, this was all he needed. He shot a look at Juliet, sure she'd have more confidence now, but she had sunk even further into her chair.

"George." Jonathon walked over to him, holding his hand out. "What can Rob get you to drink?"

"Black coffee please, Rob." George shot back his cuff to check his watch. "I don't have long, due on a teleconference in half an hour. Bring me up to date."

Jonathon nodded his thanks to Rob, dismissing him. "Juliet?" Juliet shook her head.

"Right then, George, time to tell you what your daughter has planned. She has booked Marcus Longbottom to help with the Gala Dinner, and apparently the BBC food crew are all set to come out here…tomorrow, is it, Juliet?"

Juliet nodded, without looking up at either of them. The mandarin was being subjected to a very thorough scrutiny.

"Booked?" George sat down beside his daughter and bent his head to hers.

"Yes, Daddy. I thought it was what you wanted, all that lovely publicity." Juliet raised her eyes to him and Jonathon inwardly groaned. She worked the puppy dog eyes on her dear ole daddy, and from what Jonathon had seen already, George would fall for it. Damn. There was no going back with the BBC, and in fact, it was a pretty good idea. If only she had checked with him beforehand. But there may be a way to use this to his advantage. At least now, George could see that she couldn't be trusted to the role of exec.

George paced around the small boardroom.

Juliet straightened her shoulders and sat up straighter. "It is a good idea, Daddy. I know publicity and at the moment, Marcus Longbottom is *the* chef to have here."

George looked at Jonathon. "What do you think?"

"Well, not allowing for the fact that I have an extremely competent and highly creative head chef already, it is a good idea, certainly. But it doesn't mask the fact that Juliet saw fit to book this without checking with me. I think you both must see that I cannot have an exec on my board with such clear insubordination." Out of the corner of his eye, he saw George nodding.

"What experience do you have anyway, Juliet?" She shook her

head once, and then rested it in her hand, the very picture of glumness.

"Well then, I propose that you start out as a PR junior manager. We have a very good PR manager based in Sydney, where I would like you to be based to learn the trade." He held up a hand to stop Juliet from interrupting. "I know you know the business, but you clearly do not know how to work *within* a business."

"I think that may be a good idea." George stood still, arms folded.

Juliet erupted from her chair. "Do you honestly think I'd be happy to work as a nobody? Daddeeeeee!" Her voice ended up as a wail.

Jonathon hid a smile. "What did you have in mind, seeing as an exec position is out of the question?"

Juliet pouted, and thought, one finger tapping her lip. "Well, how about I be the go-between for our corporation and your company? That way I can learn to work within a business, so I can be PR exec, say, this time next year."

PR exec, in your dreams, honey. "Well..." Jonathon walked to the doors onto the balcony and stared outside. "I'm not sure I could trust you, or your judgement. That's a very senior role you're asking for."

"Now look here." George frowned at him. "That's my daughter you're talking about."

"Yes, but as you know, Juliet wants me to fire my best chef. How can I trust her not to make demands anytime she takes a dislike to someone?"

"Oh, it's not because I dislike her." Juliet changed tack now to a wheedling tone. "I think she's really good."

"Oh great, so I need to fire her then." Jonathon wanted to smack a hand over his mouth, for sarcasm had found its way in despite his best efforts. Fortunately, neither George nor Juliet seemed to notice. Juliet was sticking her bottom lip out in a good imitation of a toddler about to throw her toys out of her pram.

"Oh, all right then, I only said that because I wanted to make room for Marcus." She muttered something else.

"Right then." Jonathon ignored the mutterings. It was probably something to do with her and Pippa and he really didn't want to know, thank you very much. He just wanted to get this damn deal signed without losing Pippa.

"We have a deal then? The Stevenson Corporation and Queen Cruises are going into business together. We keep Pippa, and Juliet comes on board as relationship manager between our two companies. She will work closely with the PR team with the view of becoming exec in the future. Regarding the Gala Dinner, that is a mistake you made that I shall have to sort out. Somehow. Deal?" He stuck out his hand.

George smiled and shook his hand hard. "Deal. Juliet?"

"Great, it's a deal." Juliet too shook his hand, with a wet fish kind of a handshake. She half looked at Jonathon. "Does this mean we'll be seeing lots more of each other?" She reached over and straightened his tie.

"It does, but obviously, any relationship couldn't be anything other than purely professional. Just to protect both our names, you understand." Juliet looked as though she were about to sulk again. "Anyway, you've got Marcus coming over."

"I sure do, honey, except he's only interested in some ex-girlfriend who dumped him and left London. Still, maybe I could take his mind off her. She's an ex for a reason, after all."

"No better woman, Juliet." It was nice to be able to relax around her, now that the relationship was strictly on a professional basis.

A thought raced through him. What had she said about Marcus Longbottom pining after an ex? That couldn't be Pippa, could it? She had worked with him, after all. Was she going out with him when working with him? No, surely not, not after all she had said to him.

Chapter Twelve

"Pippa? Pippa!" The kitchen had just sent out the last main course, and Pippa was in the sweets cold room checking on the desserts when she heard Rob calling her. She washed her hands and went into the main kitchen.

"I'm here, what's the panic? Does the redoubtable Doubtful need something else?"

"No, they're all finished, Eagleton said to tell you the food was good. But wait 'til you hear what they were talking about." He took a mushroom canapé and leaned against the counter, crossing his ankles.

Pippa leaned up beside him. "Ooooh, have you some juicy gossip?"

"I do." Rob lowered his voice conspiratorially. "But I think Eagleton clocked the fact that I was listening, so if he finds out that anybody knows, he'll know it came from me. Maybe I shouldn't say." He gave her a sideways grin, clearly delighting in his newfound knowledge.

"I won't tell anybody. Come on, spill!" She leaned her shoulder up against him as her stomach lurched. Was she going to like what he was about to tell her?

"Weeeell..." Rob pretended to deliberate. "Juliet Stevenson and Eagleton are in cohorts together!" The words came out in a rush.

"What?" Juliet and Jonathon, together? Of course, a match made in heaven. No wonder Jonathon had looked so guilty on the morning after the hut. He had been cheating on Juliet. A shiver ran through her, drawing her shoulders in as though to protect her heart.

133

"I just overheard Juliet talking about being on the board of executives, can you imagine it?"

"Wait a minute." Pippa put a hand to her forehead and absentmindedly stroked it. "Are they *together*? Or just in business together?" Please let it be the latter.

"Oh, business, I guess, although—" Rob stopped when he saw her face. "Are you okay?" He slipped an arm around her, and gently squeezed her shoulder.

"Fine, I just haven't eaten much today." She blew a long breath out between pursed lips. *It's okay, he's not with her.* Her heart recovered and the deafening sound subsided beat by beat.

"So how do you mean, in business?"

"I *think*, and again, don't quote me, she's going to be on the board of execs as PR exec."

"But has she ever worked before? That's crazy." Although it was a darn sight better than her original conclusion.

"To tell you the truth, I don't think Jonathon was too happy about it. He certainly looked pissed off to me."

"That may explain why he's been going around looking so stressed. I know he was keen to get the deal signed, so perhaps she being on the board was part of it. PR exec, hey? Well that's far enough away on the chain of command not to affect our work, so that's a relief. Now, I need something to eat."

"Some canapés, m'lady?" Rob bowed low, gesturing to his trolley of food.

Pippa laughed, the relief that Jonathon wasn't involved with Juliet making itself known in a clear bubble that emerged as a giggle.

"Get on with you, Rob." She swatted him with her towel. "I don't need any disruptions. I can't believe the Gala Dinner is tomorrow night and I've got loads to do!" Thank God for the distraction it provided, stopping her obsessing about Jonathon. Perhaps she had been a bit harsh on him but in her opinion, a man lays himself wide open when he says he thinks a woman only gets to the top by sleeping with her boss. However, there was a niggling voice telling her that she was only trying to justify herself. She knew she was super-touchy on the subject due to being the butt of jokes when working and sleeping with Marcus.

"You'll be great, I know you will. I'll ensure the restaurant staff is on top form as well. It'll be a fantastic night."

"I hope so. I'm still a bit nervous about it though. Fingers crossed for me, hey." Pippa felt under siege when she thought about the enormity of the task that lay ahead of her. It was the first time she would be sending out such a large quantity of high-quality food. Each two hundred plates of the five courses, plus their accompanying side dishes, had to be brought out together on time and hot, and sent out as fast as possible. Pippa had requested extra waiting staff, as she preferred to send the food out already plated instead of silver served—ensuring, as long as there were enough staff, everything would be served piping hot.

She had it all under control. Each chef in the kitchen was fully briefed as to what was expected of them. The food was being delivered in the morning, and once she had checked that everything was present and correct, she could relax a smidgen.

Then it would be full on for the rest of the day, and she was already anticipating the champagne at the end of service, signalling a successful night. Big nights like these were the business. The adrenaline would be pumping as they found a rhythm and ran with it, culminating in a priceless feeling of success and camaraderie within the team.

First, she had to get through the busy hours before she started mentally congratulating herself. Singing to herself, she went to get her plan of order and headed up on deck to see the beautiful Dusky Fiord laid out before her, a surreal image.

Ancient glaciers had carved the valleys out of the mountains, leaving very steep slopes down to the water. It was prehistoric—

she could imagine dinosaurs like Nessy the Loch Ness monster, slinking their long necks out of the water to eat the thick forestry that grew on either side. It was breath-taking, unlike anything she had encountered before.

She drank it in from both sides and she saw herself walking the Dusky Trail, an errant mind throwing in the picture of Jonathon at her side.

She hauled her thoughts back, examining them intently. Perhaps it was the simple beauty of the scenery pulling honesty from her, maybe she tired of pretending, possibly it was a mixture of both. But she could see clearly now that Jonathon occupied a little place in her heart, warming her from within.

This was scary stuff. Was she in love with him? Could she be with him for the rest of her life? Would she be ready to turn her back on single life? Stripping back all pretence, her heart picked up the pace.

Yes. Jonathon is the one. Oh. My. God.

Of course Jonathon was at her side in her daydream, he was her soul mate. Surely if she felt this strongly, he must feel something for her. Damn damn damn. Did he? What did he think of her? Oh, this was too much. Backtrack, fast, *forgeddaboudit.*

To business. The dinner tomorrow night. Breathing a deep breath of the clear air, she bent her head and immersed herself in her work, determined not to think of anything else.

*

Jonathon strode through the kitchen, scanning right to left looking out for Pippa. She had to be here somewhere. Seeing Christian, the kitchen porter washing the floors, he walked up to him.

"Christian, hi, how's it going?"

"Great, thanks, Mr. Eagleton."

"How did the evening's service go?"

"Very well. Chef had me preparing the vegetables. She thinks I'll be ready to start my training in no time at all." Christian went pink with the pleasure of telling the CEO his success.

"That's great, Christian, I'm pleased." Jonathon put a hand on the boy's shoulder and smiled at him. He wasn't all that different in age as Jonathon had been when he had been given his first break. "Where is the chef now?"

The boy frowned, leaning on his broom. "I'm not sure, I saw her talking to Rob earlier, and I haven't seen her since. Have you tried the office?"

"I'll go and check there. Thanks, and good for you. Well done." With a nod to him, Jonathon went to the kitchen office, only to see it empty. He stopped, disgruntled, and ran his fingers through his hair. He didn't have time to chase after her, there was a lot of work waiting for him before the BBC arrived tomorrow.

Perhaps someone in the staff canteen may know where she was. *Yeah, with Rob.* He pushed the thought out of his mind, but it left an image of the two of them together in its wake. He shook his head in annoyance as he strode down the corridor to the staff canteen.

He heard Fiona's voice before he rounded the corner and she nearly bumped into him.

"Hi Fiona, I'm looking for Pippa, do you know where she is?" he wasted no time on pleasantries, just wanting to find Pippa.

"Nope, 'fraid not. I've just come from our room and she wasn't there either."

"Did she have any plans to go ashore, do you know?"

"I doubt it. She's pretty excited about the dinner tomorrow night, and I know she had lots to get sorted beforehand."

Jonathon felt a pang of shame. All right, so it wasn't his fault that tomorrow night was being taken from Pippa, but he wasn't looking forward to seeing her face fall when he told her.

"I need to see her, urgently. If you see her, will you tell her I'm in the Doubtful and to please come and see me?"

"Sure thing, Mr E." Fiona smiled at him and stepped over the threshold of the canteen door.

With the door swinging shut behind her, he put a hand to his forehead. Where else could she be? The engine noise of the ship started idling, and Jonathon knew it was preparing to stop. Perhaps she was on deck, watching the fiords. *Of course!*

Honestly, sometimes he felt so dim. He should have gone straight up on deck.

Taking the steps two at a time, he arrived up on deck just in time to see the sun slide behind the mountains and darkness come in to tuck the ship up for the night. The last remaining pink and orange clouds took on a purple hue, giving away to charcoal grey, and dispersed to present the stars. He didn't move, didn't even breathe, glad of the unexpected peace and quiet.

He took a couple of deep breaths and checked the deck for her. There were plenty of customers enjoying the view but no flame-haired girl to be seen. Perhaps it was just as well, the romantic setting and sun going down had put him in a sentimental mood, not good considering the information he had to impart. Pippa sure as hell wasn't going to like his news, and who knew how she was going to react. All he knew was that he wanted to be the one to tell her and comfort her if she became upset. He sighed. So much for trying to make himself feel better.

Cursing to himself, he made his way through the crowds down to the stern.

"Jonathon, hi." He heard Stevenson call his name. "Come and have a cigar with me."

"Love to, George, but there's a lot to be done for tomorrow. Save it 'til the fireworks?"

George gave him the thumbs up. Reaching the stern, Pippa was still nowhere to be found. Circling around back to the deck, he stopped and looked out over the still water. How could she disappear on a ship? There were a finite number of places she had to be, so where was she? She had to be told about Marcus coming tomorrow and by him only.

If she found out by someone other than him, she would be royally pissed off. Perhaps he should write her a letter. Nah, that was just stupid, she wouldn't even bother to read it. He tapped a finger against his lips. Still, it was worth a go. Despite a desire to stay here and watch the scenery, listen to the rhythm of the waves and the wind, he had to carry on looking for her. And perhaps when he was in the Doubtful writing it, she may hear he was looking for her and come down. Here's hoping.

*

Once she heard his footsteps recede, Pippa let go of the breath she had been holding, easing her aching lungs. She had positioned herself on a lifejacket box under the lifeboats, in an attempt to avoid the customers, namely Juliet Stevenson. Her emotions felt raw after her epiphany earlier on and she knew that Juliet's smug face may be the thing to push her over the edge. Nothing whatsoever to do with the fact that she couldn't bear seeing Jonathon without wanting to be close to him.

Upon smelling his unique smell, that sea pine spice scent, close her heart had clutched at her chest and started yammering. If he were her soul mate, he would have heard the internal drum of her heart and soul and turned to see her.

But after a pause, he had moved on. Well, he was gone now, so at least she could distract herself with her work again. It was lovely and quiet here, and Pippa decided there and then to make it her office, her little hidey hole. Talk about an office with a view.

Several hours later, the cold fingering its way through her clothes, Pippa uncurled herself. Sitting up, she stretched up to the Milky Way. *Hi, Southern Cross.* All of her work was finished for the night, she had written out plans and timings for each station in the kitchen, and there was no more she could do until the food arrived in the morning.

Time for a hot chocolate, and maybe she'd be naughty and pop a whisky in it. Pure medicinal purposes, as she wanted a good sleep without worrying what the next evening may bring.

Fiona was asleep by the time she got back to their room with her drink, and Pippa crept around their room getting ready for bed with only the light from the crack of the ajar door to go by. The faint taste of whisky cutting through the creamy hot chocolate was heavenly, and Pippa found she didn't miss her nightly read as sleep soon came to claim her.

*

Jonathon wasn't quite tearing his hair out, but he was close. Pippa was damned elusive. The thought had crossed his mind that perhaps she had jumped ship, but it was quickly banished. Her professionalism, and he smiled as he thought of it, wouldn't allow her to do so.

The BBC were on their way. Juliet had texted him to say they would arrive at six a.m., but she didn't know if Marcus Longbottom was accompanying them or arriving on his own. They had a meet and greet session upon arrival, and if he couldn't find Pippa beforehand then hopefully she would be at work by the time the meeting was over. He had written her a letter, and in it he had told her about Marcus arriving. Not being sure of what else to say, he had played safe by asking her to see him as soon as possible. If there was too much information and the letter got into the wrong hands, it could jeopardise the deal.

I just hope she lets me explain.

*

Pippa's inner alarm went off, awakening her bright and early. Five-thirty a.m. Yikes, she was early, but she knew excitement and nerves wouldn't let her sleep in. Fiona slumbered on beside her, oblivious to the fact that this was the most exciting day of Pippa's career. Pippa was tempted to shake her awake, but reason stopped her. She grabbed her shower gear and her clothes for the day, and padded down the empty corridor toward the bathroom, thanking her lucky stars there wasn't a queue to face at this hour of the morning. Taking advantage of the fact that no one was waiting, she washed and conditioned her hair, something she did only rarely as it took up so much time, and couldn't be done if there were fellow staff members outside. The day ahead was going to be long and busy, and the makeup would no doubt slide down her face by mid-morning, but she applied it with a shaky hand. May as well look her best.

She took the stairs to the kitchen two at a time, her mind cycling through the agenda. First thing was to meet with her second chef, Alfonso, and go through the day with him. She tunelessly whistled through her teeth as she went around turning on the kitchen's florescent lights. Oh, she loved her job, and the frissons of excitement that snaked their way through her. The smell of freshly percolated coffee rose in the air and soon Alfonso came into view, yawning, but holding two cups of coffee.

"Your morning coffee, Pippa."

"Thanks, Alfonso, you're a gem. This will, no doubt, be the first of many today. Come on, let's head into the office, I've got your copy of the plans with me."

As they sat there chatting through the day, confidence took a firm hold. She was in control. Everything was fine. They'd be celebrating the most successful Gala Dinner ever tonight. No question of it.

Seeing movement out of her peripheral vision, she turned to Alfonso. "Excellent, it looks as though the breakfast chefs are turning up. Let's go and see about the deliveries."

"Sure thing, boss." Alfonso stuck his hand out to her. "It's going to be a good day." He shook her hand vigorously and smiled at her as they stepped out of the office.

"Hang on, I forgot my clipboard." Pippa turned to go back and stopped dead. Her tired mind was playing tricks on her.

There, in front of her, was Marcus.

Chapter Thirteen

She blinked.

She shook her head.

Perhaps her mind was too worn out. Maybe it was recalling the last time she had a big exciting day ahead of her when working with Marcus. She closed her eyes, held them closed, and then opened one a fraction to peer out. It was no good. He was still there.

Her tummy flipped over. What on earth was happening? Was he here to find her, to tell her it had all been a mistake and he wanted her back? Surely not. Thoughts swirled, each one clamouring for her attention.

"Pippa, it's mighty good to see you." Marcus held out his arms as though to encase her in a hug. She took a step backwards, clutching her coffee cup for dear life. Alfonso looked at her, and stepped half in front of her.

"Hi, I'm Marcus." He put a hand out to Alfonso, who ignored it.

"I know who you are, but I don't see what you're doing in Pippa's kitchen."

Yeah, Alfonso, you tell him. Marcus was looking smooth, almost as though he'd had botox injected in his forehead, and his clothes hung on a body that clearly had been working out since the last time she had seen him.

"Don't you know? Pippa?" Marcus looked past Alfonso to her, his forehead doing funny things in an effort to frown. She cleared her throat, and tried to take her gaze from it.

"No, Marcus, but I'm hoping you will enlighten us."

The cockiness left his stance, and he looked small. "Well, I'm here to cater—" He cut off as the sound of people talking came to them, clearly coming this way. Pippa heard Jonathon's voice, and she had a sense of being behind a fuzzy screen, watching everything going on and being helpless to stop it or to leave. Similar to a lucid dream and she shivered under the bright lights.

Jonathon and Juliet rounded the corner, arguing.

"You told me six a.m., you exasperating woman." He stopped short upon seeing them, and Juliet nearly ran into the back of him.

"Ow, watch...oh. Hi everyone, Marcus," Juliet said. Pippa had never heard Marcus name's being said with such a predatory purr, and she watched in disbelief as Juliet reached over and planted a lingering kiss on his cheek. This was getting more bizarre by the second.

"Have you been introduced to Pippa?" Juliet had a look of triumph on her face that heightened Pippa's sense of impending disaster and sent her flipped tummy through the floor.

"We know each other." Marcus spoke quietly, his blue eyes on Pippa.

"Marcus, darling," Juliet gazed at him with adoration, and frowned when she saw the direction his look had taken, "agreed to come over to cook for the Gala Dinner this evening."

Pippa shook her head minutely and blinked. The fuzzy screen turned to high definition. With the sound muted. She looked around at them in slow motion. Alfonso looked confused, Juliet exultant, Marcus was unsure, and Jonathon...it was when she saw Jonathon that she knew. He gazed at her, concern turning his tawny eyes velvet, and looking deeper into his eyes, she saw guilt. It was true. Dammit. Damn him. Damn them all. Tears threatened but she would be damned herself if she let them loose.

She flung her tea-towel over her shoulder and turned on the heels of her chef's clogs. Jonathon moved quickly, to be at her shoulder.

"I can explain," he said in a low voice to her.

She stopped, and lifted her head up with an effort. "It doesn't matter."

"Pippa." It was Marcus. "When I heard about this publicity stunt, I jumped at it. I couldn't wait to see you again. You look fantastic." He reached out again to her, and once more she stepped out of his reach. She tried to unscramble her brain, but the thoughts were too slippery for her to get a grip.

"Pardon? Oh, you too, Marcus. I'll be back in a minute, I just need to check on something." How she'd managed to come out with something coherent was beyond her. Jonathon fell into step beside her as she moved away. When they had gone out of earshot, she stopped, her body feeling too heavy to move.

"What the hell is he doing here? Is this some kind of sick joke?" She rounded on him, feeling the fire gather in her belly and welcoming it in the hope it would turn her disappointment to ash.

Jonathon massaged his temples but gazed at her intently.

"No, it's not. I'm sorry, this was set up without my assent or even knowledge."

"I thought you were the CEO, in control of everything on board this ship." She spat the words at him, yet even as she said them, the heat of the moment started to depart her, leaving congealed disappointment behind.

"It's not that simple," Jonathon said.

She gazed down the corridor, not hearing him. *Her wonderful day, all over before it had begun.*

"Pippa, please listen to me. I didn't know—"

To her horror, she felt the tears gathering, constricting her throat. *Hold it together, just for now. I can do that at least.* But she had to get out of there before she fell apart.

"Don't make it worse." Her voice rose on the last word and she wrapped her arms around herself.

"I just want to explain," Jonathon said.

"Okay. But not now. I need to grab five minutes to myself."

She stopped, needing to breathe in the hope that mere oxygen could sustain her through the next few seconds. "Just to make sure I've got it straight, though, Marcus Longbottom is here to cook for the Gala Dinner tonight? I'm not required?"

"Of course you are, it couldn't be done without you."

Baloney.

"But to all intents and purposes, for the sake of better *publicity*, Marcus is cooking." Pippa ran a hand over her face, pressing her forefinger and thumb into the corner of her eyes, damming the tears. She kept her eyes closed.

"Only for the publicity, yes."

"Fine. Give me some time, then you know where you can find me." Drawing strength from the upcoming solitude, she looked fully at him, the resulting physical jolt shocking her with its intensity. Tenderness was written all over his face for her. It seemed like he...he *cared* for her.

"Great, I'll bring the coffee." Relief rang loud and clear in his words. "And Pippa, just let me say one thing." He reached out a hand to cup her face and stroked her cheek with his thumb.

All her senses culminated in her face, all the better to feel his touch but somehow, with a mammoth internal struggle, she managed not to turn to the warmth and submerge herself in it.

"I'm sorry this has happened. I didn't mean it to, I promise you."

"Sure." The word shook and she turned before the world followed suit, for wracking sobs were on the horizon and advancing fast. "I'll see you soon."

The corridor she walked down seemed to go on forever, the walls closing in. *Don't think, just put one foot in front of the other.* As she passed through the staff accommodation, she heard Fiona's laugh from behind a closed door. She must have gone to see David, who shared his room with the chefs, and so their own room would be empty.

Her bed called to her, and the thought of burying herself beneath the duvet and giving into her despair appealed greatly. But the knowledge that someone, sooner or later, would come looking for her gave her the strength to resist. She sat on the edge, gnawing on her thumbnail. She felt like a little girl, with Christmas cancelled. It was too much. Tears escaped to spill silently down her cheeks, a steady stream to rival the Queen Elizabeth Falls outside.

Yet an answer glistened through her befuddled brain. Leave then. Leave it all behind her. But go where? Oh who cares, just get out of here. Getting up, she struggled out of her chef's whites and flung on her jeans and jumper. It was then she saw the envelope, on the ground, where the door must have pushed it. Her name was written on it, in strong, bold print, and, hand shaking, she opened it.

Dear Pippa, I've been looking all over for you. Marcus Longbottom is on his way over here, to increase our much-needed publicity tomorrow. I need to talk to you about it so when you get this, would you please, whatever the time is, come to the Doubtful so I can explain? J.

She ran her fingers over the script. His writing was like him: strong, no nonsense, and arrogant. *Sorry, Pippa, you're just not good enough for our Gala Dinner, so we're flying over your ex-boss to put things right.*

In an effort to stem the tears she promised herself a good cry when she was away from here, and packed the last of her things. With a final look at the cabin, she hoisted her bag on her shoulder and shut the door. *Don't think, just do.* Hopefully the Xplorer would be making a trip inland to take the customers who wanted to kayak in the sound into bay.

She kept her head down as she walked, the last thing she wanted was to run into someone she knew. Although a small part of her yearned to be stopped and to have her decision taken out of her hands. Was she right to go? Would the kitchen handle the dinner without her? What about Jonathon? The realization she had come to last night? Could she not stay and talk, at least, to him?

Images of an entwined Marcus and Juliet, the big dinner, her team, and Jonathon being too busy to even notice she was gone struck up a cinematic loop. Everything else she could handle, but Jonathon's lack of respect for her, both as a chef and as a woman, swung the balance and she stepped aboard the Xplorer just in time for it to move away from the Coral Princess.

She brought her knees up to her chest and laid her head down on them, not wanting to see the Xplorer taking her away. Just an hour ago, she had been full of excitement and dreams of her future as a bright up and coming chef. Walking through life with Jonathon at her side. It was all shattered.

*

Jonathon strode through the kitchen for the umpteenth time, scattering agitation like a flower girl scattering rose petals.

"Where is she?" he barked at Alfonso.

"Not here. Sorry, Mr. Eagleton, she hasn't come back yet."

Jonathon ran his hands through his hair, absentmindedly giving himself a small head massage as he did so. *Think, man, think. She has to be somewhere. She wouldn't just leave all her hard work behind.*

"Alfonso, did she let you know how she was going to run the dinner?" A suspicion was starting to take shape.

Alfonso gave him a big smile, misinterpreting Jonathon's fear. "Not to worry, she briefed me in full about the entire day. She even wrote her instructions for each station down, and gave me the master copy, whilst giving each station their own. Pippa leaves nothing to chance, she's such a good chef."

Yes, yes but where was she? The answer Alfonso gave sparked his suspicions into flame.

"Fine. Where's Fiona?"

"She'll be in her office, at reception on the first floor." Alfonso had to raise his voice as Jonathon had already left the kitchen.

He walked quickly through the corridor, shooting back his cuff to look at his Breitling. She had been gone forty-five minutes by now. A niggle inside his gut started to move up to his heart. She must be here. She had disappeared last night, only to reappear again. So maybe she would do the same again today.

But his suspicions refused to listen to reason. He had seen the way devastation had etched itself clearly on her face when she had asked him for a little time alone. Disillusionment shone dully from her normally sparkling green eyes, and she had deflated before his eyes. Pippa, the girl who had an answer for everything, who surrounded herself with fun, who had a temper like an alley cat, her light had gone out.

The memory of her white, strained face tried to pull his heart into his abdomen. He wanted to enfold her in his arms and smooth the rigidity from her shoulders. Kiss her eyelids gently to restore the sparkle to her eyes, and slide his lips down to the corner of her mouth and breathe love into her. Watch the roses bloom in her cheeks again, and have her worry melt away like a butterfly.

Oh, to have her safe in his arms, as she was in his heart. He loved this girl. He acknowledged the thought with little surprise, as if he had always known it. *Jonathon Eagleton loves Pippa Renshaw.* It was familiar to him, as though he had written it in the stars.

The door to Fiona's office was open. "Fiona?" he called as he pushed it wide. "Good, you're here," he said to the top of her head as she was poring over some files.

"Hi, Mr. E, what's up?" She was light and breezy.

"Have you seen Pippa this morning?" Jonathon dove straight into the conversation. He knew he was being rude, but he just wanted to see Pippa and make sure she was okay.

"Not yet, I know she's very busy and don't expect we'll touch base unless I head into the kitchen looking...what?" She broke off as Jonathon held a hand up.

"Would you mind checking your room?"

"Course not, but what's the problem?"

"I'll walk with you, fill you in on the way."

Fiona had to trot beside Jonathon's long gait, but he took no notice and started talking as soon as they left the office. When she heard that Pippa had bumped into Marcus, Fiona stopped dead in her tracks. Jonathon carried on walking and talking until he reached their room and there was no Fiona with him. Glancing back, he saw her with her hand to her mouth.

"Pardon me, Mr. Eagleton, but are you telling me that Marcus Longbottom is here to take over the kitchen for the Gala Dinner and she had absolutely no idea until she bumped into him this morning in her kitchen?"

"That's what I'm saying."

"Poor Pippa." Fiona glared at him, blame written all over her face and nearly pushed him over in her haste to get to their cabin. Flinging the door open, she stood in the doorway, scanning her room.

"She was here." Fiona stepped into her room, and upon opening the cupboard, discovered it empty of Pippa's clothes.

"But?"

"She's gone, and she's taken all her stuff with her." Fiona sat on Pippa's neatly made bed.

Jonathon ran his hands through his hair. "I'm checking the Xplorer, although I think it's left by now. Walk with me again please."

"Sure thing. You don't think she's left the ship?"

"Looks that way. Did she say anything to you about where she may go?" Jonathon was short, but his mind was busy whirling through the possibilities. Where would she go?

"No. I haven't seen her since yesterday afternoon, when all she was talking about was the Gala Dinner this evening. I can't believe you brought Marcus Longbottom over to run it instead." Her voice was accusing. "Talk about a kick in the teeth."

"It wasn't planned, if that makes you feel any better."

"Well, I'm sure it wouldn't make Pippa feel any better. That must have been some shock this morning."

"Well, yes, I can't imagine she was overjoyed to see her ex-boss here to take over her kitchen."

"Not just her ex-boss, either." Fiona's words were coming out in huffs and puffs as she struggled to keep up with Jonathon.

"Hmm?" Jonathon's mind wasn't on the conversation; he was watching the door to the deck loom larger. Please let the boat still be here.

"Her ex-boyfriend too."

They walked through the door in time to see the toy-like Xplorer dock in the distance, at the small port in Dusky Sound. Damn.

He swung around to Fiona. "*What* did you just say?"

Fiona frowned, clearly unsure whether to repeat what she'd just said. "Marcus is Pippa's ex-boyfriend. The reason she left London." She put the words out there, floating in the air before him. Jonathon felt as though a big, invisible hand shoved him, hard, up against the door. His breath left him in a whoosh, and his eyes nearly lost themselves in the sun sparkles on the water.

"Thanks, Fiona." The words came out somehow and he didn't hear her reply as he walked off to the stern.

He gazed around at the fiords, looking for comfort. These fiords had borne witness to a hell of a lot. Standing here for millennia before white people arrived, bringing battles and bloodshed, they watched, immovable, unforgiving.

They would have seen worse than Jonathon losing Pippa, but for him it was as though all those centuries of chaos bore down on him, almost bringing him to his knees.

He raised a hand to guard against the sun and looked over to the Xplorer. He could just make out the passengers leaving it in a steady stream and he fancied he could see Pippa, stopped and looking across the expanse of water at him. *So who are you? Why didn't you let me explain? Why didn't you tell me Marcus was your ex-boyfriend?* So many damn questions. Would he ever find an answer to them? Did he want answers to them? Pippa had gotten under his skin, but he could grow a new skin, harder this time. Didn't it take seven years before all your cells regenerated to create an entirely new skin?

What about his heart, he couldn't regenerate that. Ha. He pulled a humourless smile. Perhaps a transplant could be arranged. In the meantime, he could feel a wall of ice starting to pack its way around his heart, a mother protecting her child.

He was the CEO of Queen Cruises. He had managed a deal that saved the company from certain liquidation, and had made his name one to be reckoned with in the industry. Why would he want to go messing about with love? It was far easier to remain single, unattached. Sure, it was lonely, that's what happened when you reached the top.

Fine, he was Jonathon Eagleton, he could manage it.

Chapter Fourteen

Pippa's gut wrenched as she watched the Xplorer make its way back to the ship. It had never looked so majestic, sitting in the deep waters with her engines turned off and framed against the forested cliffs. There was no going back. She was on her own in a country she didn't know and if she thought about it at all, she was going to break down.

A prearranged kayaking company met the other passengers who were soon in mini buses heading away to the kayaking centre. The port was small, with only a few single storey buildings. She glanced around for a hostel, relieved to see one just off the beaten track. No more fancy *Stevenson* hotels for her anymore, she had thrown all that away. *Don't think, just do.*

A friendly face at the desk regarded her quizzically. "Hi, I'm Mario. We have a dormitory room, or would you like a double room?"

"Double room, please." One good thing about Queen Cruises was that they paid their staff in advance. Although some of the money would now require paying back, at least she had funds to look after herself. It was the here and now that required her attention—dreaming about the future had brought little happiness.

The room shone clean and bright, much better than the room she had shared with Fiona. It had a window, complete with window seat, showing off the amazing scenery. She sat down, opened the window, and took a deep breath, pulling the air up through her diaphragm, expanding her chest. Before it reached her heart, she broke down in a sob. There wasn't enough room for air *and* tears, and the tears finally escaped and spilled silently down her cheeks.

What kind of fool was she to ever have thought that Jonathon could have loved her? To believe that she was a decent chef? To throw in a perfectly workable life in London for the dreams she had aspired to? Why had she done it to herself?

She had been so utterly excited at the thought of the Gala Dinner tonight. She loved big nights like that, and to have been in charge would, for her, have been the ultimate in job satisfaction.

Thoughts like powdery snow shifting at the top of a mountain gathered momentum as they picked up remorse and guilt, and tumbled into an avalanche of emotions. Time stood still until something became clear.

Her dreams had shattered.

*

The day should be flying past, there was enough to do: schmooze the BBC, ensure everyone was presenting their best sides to the camera, and iron out the smaller details of the new contract with Stevenson. Instead Jonathon was forever looking at his watch. The slow hand was going slower than usual, and each time he looked at his Breitling he could see Pippa's face as he had last seen her. *Stop looking at your watch then.* Thoughts like that didn't help, and come three o'clock he was ready to throw himself overboard. The constant invasion of his thoughts was driving him to near distraction, and today of all days, he couldn't afford such diversion.

Perhaps if he found out where Pippa was, then he'd be able to focus on the jobs at hand. Twice now during their meeting, Stevenson had looked at him, waiting for an answer to an unheard question.

"Sorry, George, I'm just thinking about the BBC tonight."

"Fine, as long as there are no problems?" George's eyes were keen as mustard.

"Not at all." None that were toxic, anyway.

"Really? Juliet tells me your head chef isn't here. Seems to me like she's left you in the lurch."

Jonathon's protectiveness expanded his heart and he struggled to hold back a snarl. "Not at all, quite the contrary—the kitchen, under her leadership, has never been better prepared. Marcus Longbottom has nothing to do, I hope we're not wasting money having him here." What a laugh, of course they were, but as long as the publicity paid off, it wouldn't matter in the end.

George nodded, not saying a word.

"But talking about Longbottom and the day, I have to check on how things are going with the TV crew. We're nearly done here, anyway, so let's iron out the last creases in Queenstown tomorrow."

George stood up and offered his hand.

"Good. We'll see you tonight at the Gala Dinner?"

"Certainly. I'm looking forward to it all." Jonathon shook his hand firmly, shoving away the thought of how much more enjoyable it would be if Pippa were there.

Waiting until Stevenson had left for a suitable amount of time, Jonathon headed up to the Xplorer's launching deck. He was in luck. It had just come in, the disembarking passengers taking excitedly about their kayaking.

"Lee?" He called out to the steward who worked the boat, currently sweeping up after the trip.

"Sir?"

"On the early morning trip to bay, did you see Pippa Renshaw on board?"

Lee frowned and cocked his head. "I can't say I did, Mr. Eagleton. But we were pretty busy."

Jonathon waited.

"Hang on, now that you mention it, I guess it could have been Pippa." Lee plucked at his lower lip. "I didn't recognize her, she was all huddled up. Not at all like she normally is. I remember thinking she could have been a runaway or something like that. She seemed pretty miserable."

That would have been Pippa all right.

"Did you see what she did when she got off?"

"No, I'm afraid not, I was too busy clearing up for the trip back here."

Disappointment washed over him, followed by determination. If he didn't find out where she had gone, he could kiss good-bye to this day and it was far too important a day to let that happen.

"Well, what *could* she have done?"

"Not a lot, really. She wouldn't have been able to head out with the passengers, as the buses are all fully booked." Lee's eyes opened wider. "Unless…"

"Yes, what is it?"

"There isn't much in the bay—a coffee shop and a hostel. I think—" Lee broke off, frowning deeper in concentration. "That's right, that's all there is. So she must have gone to one or the other."

"Thanks, Lee." Pulling out his iPhone, Jonathon walked to the balcony to Google hostels in the area and felt like a teenager when the search engine gave him the name and phone number of a hostel in the bay. Eureka! Unsure of what to say, he dialed and held his breath. The phone rang and rang, and he was just about to hang up when a breathless voice shouted hello.

"Yes, hi. I'm looking for an English girl who checked into your hostel this morning called Pippa Renshaw."

The voice that came back was crisp. "I'm sorry, but we can't divulge any guest information."

Jonathon ran his free hand through his hair and looked to the mountains for inspiration. "I know. And I wouldn't ask, but it's important." He wasn't sure but he thought he heard the boy on the other end snort. "I'm sorry?"

"Nothing." He was clearly laughing though.

Jonathon closed his fist and watched his knuckles turn white.

Cheeky bastard. "It is, though. It isn't exactly life or death, but it's close. I need to know if she's there."

The silence that came over the line encouraged him, so throwing caution to the mountains—which he felt sure would approve—he continued. "I had something important to say, but she ran out on me before I could tell her."

"Well, it sounds to me like she didn't want to hear it."

"Is she there?"

"I'm not saying yes, I'm not saying no. I simply can't tell you."

Jonathon swapped the phone to his other hand, and changed direction. "What's your name?"

"Mario."

"Okay, Mario, it's like this. I have had the good fortune to fall in love with a wonderful woman. She is also irrepressible and aggravating, but it's this that makes her irresistible. Have you ever felt like that about a woman?" *Please God let him know what I'm talking about.*

"Hey, I sure did. I married her though; I didn't send her running for the hills." Mario sounded pleased with himself.

"Then you know how I feel. Please Mario, just let me know she's there. That's all I want to know."

There was a pause. Jonathon watched the Queen Elizabeth Falls thundering down the cliff side, resulting in a tremendous steam rising from the lakes.

"Oh okay, then."

"Okay what?"

"She's here, she checked in this morning. But I tell you, she did not look happy, her pretty face all creased up. You'd better be good to her."

"I will." Jonathon promised it before thinking. "Mario, thanks."

He disconnected, and gazed blankly at his screen. Right, now he knew she was safe, he could go about his day. He grimaced, and rocked back on his heels. Focus, busy day. Go to work.

"Mr. Eagleton?" Fiona had come up on deck, looking for him.

"Hi, Fiona. What's up?" Good, time to work.

"Juliet apparently told Marcus's crew that they could all stay on board tonight..." Fiona was smart enough to keep her opinions to herself, but disbelief was written all over her face.

"And of course, we have no room," Jonathon finished off her sentence, all the while wondering what would have happened had Mulberry still been here. The company would have fallen to pieces, with both him and Juliet Stevenson making rash promises.

"Okay. I guess we can't make up beds for them in the ballroom?"

"Only problem with that, Mr. E., is that the ballroom is in use."

Jonathon slapped his hand against the side of his head. "Of course it is. Right then, here—" he flicked through his dialed numbers "—is the number for the hostel on the shore, the guy's name is Mario. Tell him to say thanks, I'm sending over...how many are there?"

"Ten."

"I'm sending over ten customers for the night. Hang on, how about Marcus himself?" He couldn't send him over there, not to where Pippa was.

"Em...I don't think his accommodation will be a problem."

Jonathon looked at her and experienced an eerie sense of déjà vu. "Oh yes?"

"I think Juliet will take care of that, if you see what I mean."

Clearly, Mulberry and Juliet had a lot more in common than he had originally thought. Perhaps he should introduce them, Pippa would find it hilarious. *Stop!*

"Is there anything else, Fiona?" He looked back over to where he imagined the hostel to be, holding his lips together in a crooked smile.

"Actually, yeah. Has Pippa left for good, do you think?"

Air gushed from his lungs and he took a deep breath of the lake's clean air, gathering his words. "I hope not, perhaps she may be persuaded to come back but for now we should assume she's not." He glanced sideways at Fiona, expecting her expression to be mirroring his of gloom. Instead, she stood there with one hand on her hip, the other clutching the ubiquitous clipboard to her chest, with fire in her eyes.

"Her running away is totally understandable, that was a rotten thing for anyone to go through. But I believe you could get her back."

Jonathon frowned and opened his mouth to ask her what she meant, but her pager started beeping and without looking at it, she turned it off. "It'll be Ann, my second in command. Must go and get those rooms sorted. Thanks, Mr. Eagleton." She hurried off down the stairs into the main body of the ship, leaving Jonathon out on deck.

Go get her.

Would he? Should he? Admitting his love for her was easy in comparison to this. Yes, of course he was going to get her, dammit. He wasn't going to let her walk out of his life. As soon as he could get away, he was across that water, going to get her.

*

A gentle breeze came through the open window. Pippa sniffed and turned her face outwards, toward the breeze. A heady smell of pine and loam came through the open window. Pippa drew a shuddering breath and turned her face outward, toward the gentle breeze.

The mountains loomed close, beckoning. All right, so her dream of climbing them with Jonathon wasn't about to come true, so she may as well get on with walking them on her own. She could probably buy some hiking food at the front desk, and a strong coffee to help her attack those ascents. Her heart rose. If anything would help, it would be a day out in these beautiful surroundings.

Mario was the only person in the small office. Clearly business was slow.

"Hi, Mario, do you sell scroggin? And do you have maps of the walks in the area?"

"We sure do. If you look behind you, they're on the wall. Choose which walk you'd like to do and if you need it, I'll sell you the corresponding ordinance survey map. Depends on how long you want to go for. The short walks are easily sign-posted."

Pippa stood, tried to make sense of the entire wall covered in treks. "I only want a four, maybe five-hour max trip."

Mario leaned on the reception counter, eyes alight as he described the places within easy distance. As she watched and listened, a yearning for the simple life unfurled. A life in which she had never heard of Jonathon Eagleton, nor had any grandiose ideas of being a head chef aboard a luxury cruise liner, going places.

Hah. Forget that.

How lovely instead would it be to live here, to kayak and hike whenever your heart so desired. She'd become the most relaxed person in the world. Yet there was a little niggle at the back of her brain. The one that said she *needed* the thrill of working, savoured the rush of being around Jonathon. But then it wasn't as if she had a choice, now was it?

She exhaled a long breath and blew a curl from her face.

"Great, Mario, whatever you think is best, I trust your judgment." She smiled, setting her tiredness behind her.

"You can't go far wrong." He smiled at her. "Em…"

"Yes?"

"Oh nothing. I mean, here's your scroggin. Right then." He glanced at the clock behind him. "It's eleven a.m., I'll expect you back before four p.m., otherwise I'll start to worry. That gives you five hours to do an easy three-hour hike. Think you can manage it?"

Pippa picked an apple from the bowl on the desk, threw it up in the air, and caught it smoothly. "Easy. Thanks, Mario, see you then."

See, her heart had lifted just by making a small effort, and the walking would help to keep it from the doldrums. Great to be finally out in the open. She deliberately kept her back to the far off Coral Princess but couldn't stop her mind harking to it.

So, eleven a.m....

The kitchen should have taken delivery of all the food, it had better all be there. Christian would be busy preparing the vegetables, he had a talent, that boy. Alfonso would be in his element, walking around, telling everybody what to do, but with an easygoing humour that endeared him to many of the staff.

And Jonathon, what would he be doing? Her chest contracted. Damn the man, he now had a place in her mind as well as her heart. Hewn into her mind like the Hollywood sign, only there was nothing glamorous about unrequited love. Had he missed her? Trying to stop herself from thinking about Jonathon was like trying to stop the waterfalls thundering over the cliffs. Perhaps she should just let her mind think about him, just this once. Call it a mourning process, a wake. She'd walk and think about him, and when she returned to the hostel, employ strict discipline and put him clean out of her mind. And her heart.

Her spirits rose infinitesimally just at the thought of being able to dwell on him, that last look of his as she left him. His face had been gentle in tenderness, eyes deepening in a warm caress as he had reached to her. If she allowed herself, she would think that look meant something. Warmth infused the ice within her, threatening to crack it.

Just don't think of the future without him.

A few hours later, she was puffed out, standing on a ridge looking over the lakes, amazement rippling her numb emotions. Where else would you be able to do a 360-degree turn and see nothing but nature at its finest? The shadows of clouds rolling over brown mountains lined with trees and capped with snow, snugly hidden valleys and rivers. A person could be forgiven for thinking they were the only person in this world. Pippa alternatively felt small and insignificant, then strong and powerful. One moment she would scoff at her impotency, the next helplessness coursed through her.

Oh, Jonathon.

Totally enthralled in her walking, watching where her boots fell, the sight of the ship brought her right back down to earth. She had to get further away. The ship was due to depart early the next morning, and already a bereft feeling threatened to overcome her. Far better for her to leave it, and Jonathon.

But where could she go? Milford Sound? Queenstown? The ship would only haunt her if she went there.

"Peepa, come and see me." Jean-Pierre's voice popped into her head.

Could she go and see him? Just until she got things sorted out to head back to the UK? Relief flew through her at the thought of a solution, even a temporary one. That was exactly what she would do.

Call Jean-Pierre, and go back to Akoroa. Great.

Chapter Fifteen

The good thing about Juliet working for him, he didn't have to put up with her drunken ramblings and advances anymore. The ink drying on the deal helped as well. Plus, she focused her attention entirely on Marcus, positively purring whenever he came near their table.

Jonathon was free to network with the other passengers.

Free? What a joke. He didn't want to be free, he wanted Pippa on his arm. After witnessing, and thoroughly enjoying, the success that came from her kitchen for the Gala Dinner, his craving for her grew until he could almost taste it.

The night had excelled previous Gala nights, with the exception that she wasn't here to help celebrate. After he had ensured everyone was happy, Jonathon excused himself from his table and entered the brightly lit kitchen. Scenes of muted jubilation greeted him. They were all drinking the champagne he had sent through, but nobody was bubbling over with happiness. He understood it, and missed being able to celebrate a successful cruise and an even more successful deal with someone special. *Someone with corkscrew curls and bright eyes.*

Alfonso was at the coffee station. "Great night!" Jonathon held out his hand to shake his, and slapped him on the back. "Well done, the passengers were highly complimentary."

Alfonso shrugged, in a gesture lifted straight from working with Jean-Pierre. "I didn't do much. Pippa had it all organized. I just ensured it all went according to plan."

"Nonetheless, it was well done."

"Pippa should have been here, it was her night. I can't take any credit for it, although that Marcus probably will. Why wasn't she here?" Alfonso didn't smile as he spoke. "She was missed."

"Jonathon." Marcus came up behind him, slopping most of his champagne as he waved it in an expansive gesture. "How was the food?"

Alfonso interrupted. "I need to check the stores for breakfast, I must go. Mr. Eagleton, Longbottom." He nodded farewell to them both and headed into the kitchen.

Jonathon watched him go, and turned to Marcus. "Great, thanks. Alfonso here tells me that Pippa had most of it organized and there wasn't much left to do." He watched for Marcus's reaction as he said Pippa's name. To his curiosity, Marcus, even with a lot of Dutch courage inside him, couldn't meet his gaze.

"True. She did, after all, train with the best." No note of irony entered the drawled words. "So it was easy for me as she works the same way we did when we worked together. Plus I trust her so I let Alfonso run with her plan, and I just oversaw it all."

"Alfonso was just asking why she wasn't here."

"Ah. Well I think me being here made her a bit nervous."

Jonathon raised an eyebrow.

"I shouldn't say it, but…" He paused, and took a big drink out of his glass only to put it on the counter when he realized he was drinking nothing but air. "Anymore champers around?"

"What are you saying, man?" Jonathon's patience was on the wane with the drunken ex-boyfriend of the woman he loved. What on earth had Pippa seen in him?

"When we finished, I told her it was because I needed some positive publicity, the kind I could get by being linked to some of the *it* girls. Juliet, for instance. I didn't want our relationship to be over, and I'm not proud to say that I thought we could carry on in private, but be seen publicly with the girls who were in the gossip mags." His mouth drooped at the corners, and the buzz of drinking dipped without fresh supplies. "I got the publicity, but I lost the girl."

No wonder the events of this morning had thrown Pippa. Jonathon stared at Marcus, who suddenly looked sober. His gut twisted at the thought that he had said something to Pippa about Marcus being good for publicity. Dammit, she must have felt that she was being kept away from the limelight, leaving her ex-boyfriend to collect all the glory. Just like Marcus had suggested to her, back in London. History had a way of repeating itself. Poor Pippa. His heart thumped into action. *Go get her. Be with her. NOW!*

"Thanks, Marcus." Jonathon swiped the new bottle of champagne Marcus had just found, and left him standing there with a sober look of confusion on his face. *I'm coming, Pippa!*

He made a clatter running up the steel stairs to the deck. He glanced at his watch. The Xplorer wasn't due to depart until much later tonight, but he wasn't the CEO for nothing. His luck was in and the driver was there, checking the onboard computer.

"Phillip?"

"Hey, Mr. Eagleton."

"Will you take me into the bay please?"

"No problem. Shall I ask Lee to get you a drink from the bar while we're crossing?"

"No thanks, let's just go please." His desire to see Pippa was so strong it was like the sun trying to burst from his chest.

"Whatever you say, sir."

Jonathon paced around the small boat, figuring out what to say. His blood pumped through his body quickly, swirling and whirling out from his heart. Would she tell him to get lost? No doubt she thought that he had sold her out, in favour of glory. He had to make her realize that it had all been beyond his control, that she was the only girl in the world for him.

The thirty minutes it took to dock seemed to drag by, or flew past, he couldn't make up his mind which. When they stopped, he vaulted over the side without waiting for the gate to open onto the gangway. It couldn't be hard to find the hostel. He ran down the path, looking from side to side. If anyone could see him now, they'd clutch their sides in laughter. A grown man in DJ, clutching a bottle of champagne, running as though his life depended on it.

A small, warmly lit sign for the hostel appeared and he stopped dead. There it was. Pippa was less than a minute away.

He had to get a grip. Slow his heart down before he tumbled in there and made an utter fool of himself. This was worse than the most extreme caffeine overload he'd ever had. Deep breaths, in, out, in, out. Blowing the last breath through pursed lips, he crossed the gravel toward the open door.

Easy does it.

There was a young man behind the counter, frowning in concentration as he turned the pages of his book. Jonathon cleared his throat, and soon was on the receiving end of a quizzical look.

"Hi, I'm Mario. Let me guess…" He put his hand out, and Jonathon didn't like the look that came over his face. "You're looking for Pippa Renshaw, is that right?"

"Yes, I am." He shook his hand briefly. "Hi, Mario. Where is she?"

"You're too late. She's gone." Mario had a told-you-so look on his face.

"What? Where?" Jonathon put the bottle on the counter with a gratifying thump.

"She went out for a hike, then came back around four looking marginally happier, asking what, if any, buses left here today."

"And?" He had to stop himself from leaning over the counter and dragging the man up by the collar. "Tell me, man."

"One left about two hours ago."

"Where to?" His patience was about to snap.

"Queenstown."

Jonathon looked blankly at him. Queenstown, that was okay, they were heading there tomorrow after all. But that could be too late.

"When's the next one?" He checked his pockets, he had his wallet and iPhone on him, that was all he needed. There wasn't anything urgently requiring his attention back at the ship—it would be easy to meet them in Queenstown. "Well?"

Mario was just staring at him. Did he not understand his urgency? "In about twenty-two hours."

"You're kidding me." *Please be kidding me.*

"No, sorry, there's only one a day."

"Well, how can I get to Queenstown?"

Mario just shrugged.

"Is there a taxi I can call?"

"Out here? Sorry, no. Look, I told you hours ago she was here, and it took you this long to get here?"

Jonathon held back the red mist that was threatening. He had to think clearly.

"Mario, can I borrow your car?" Mario shook his head, lips in a wry smile. "I'll bring it back by six a.m., that's when the ship leaves."

"You don't understand, we don't have a car. We bike everywhere, much better for the environment."

"Motorbike?" Jonathon had a fleeting image of him roaring over the mountains to get his girl.

"Push-bike."

Poof went that image. He deflated.

"Is there any way I can get there?"

"Sure is."

"How?"

Mario came from behind the counter, and walked over to the window. "See that boat out there? I'm reliably informed she's leaving for Milford Sound at six in the morning, from where you can get a bus." Mario's words teased him from his red mist. But still, Jonathon could have throttled him, only cheerfully this time.

"I don't suppose she gave any clue as to where she may stay?"

"No, sorry." There was pity on Mario's face. "Good luck, mate, I do hope you find her. If you do, you can have your honeymoon here for free!"

"Thanks, Mario." He pushed the champagne over to him. "You and your wife may as well have that. I don't want it." He turned to walk back out the door. What was he going to do now?

Yet, the thought of a honeymoon with Pippa further softened his annoyance. He should be so lucky.

*

Pippa disconnected her phone as she walked down the high street in Queenstown, under siege from billboards and placards advertising bungee jumps, sky dives, and a multitude of other ways to part travelers and their money. If her heart were functioning properly, she would be a sucker for the adrenaline inducing experiences. Yet she had a sneaky feeling that even if she threw herself off a platform 134 metres above a river attached to an elastic band, her heart wouldn't even notice.

The bus driver had dropped her off outside a pretty hostel, just five minutes' walk away from the centre.

Jean-Pierre couldn't disguise the surprise in his voice when he'd heard Pippa on the phone.

"'ow come you are calling me, you should be finishing off your service. What is wrong?"

"I'm not there, I'm not even on board."

"Pardon?"

"Oh, Jean-Pierre, it's a long story and I'm pretty wrung out. Can I come and see you?"

His voice softened. "Mais oui. Alors Peepa, I 'ope you are okay. It breaks my 'eart that you are calling me, mais I am truly 'appy to see you again. Now, 'ow will you get here?"

"I don't know. I gather I can get a bus to Christchurch, and then make my way down to you."

Jean-Pierre tutted. "Non. Peepa, you cannot do that, you sound too sad. It will take about ten 'ours. I talk to Darrel, and call you back soon."

Pippa didn't have to wait for long before her phone beeped at her.

"Peepa, we are in luck. Darrel 'as a business associate coming 'ere tomorrow, from Queenstown, and 'e is flying 'is own airplane. 'is only a small Cessna. Will you fly with heem?"

"Course I will, that's great news. Where will I meet him?"

"Is easy to find the field, just ask anyone at your 'ostel for directions, is only a minute away from town. 'e leaves at nine a.m., and will be waiting for you."

The respite that Pippa felt started leaking through her eyes, and she sniffed. "Jean-Pierre, thank you so much. Merci beaucoup, tu es tres gentil." *You are so kind.* The tears slid down her face, stopping her from saying anything more.

"For my Peepa, nothing is too much. Now, to sleep with you, I shall see you about midday."

Pippa went back to her hostel, having little energy for checking out the nightlife, which was blessedly quiet. She made a cup of chamomile tea and went out onto the balcony to take in the night sky. Even being in a town, the stars glittered overhead, the Milky Way shining like fairy dust. Fairy dust made your dreams come true, didn't it? She sipped her tea. It would take a lot more than fairy dust to do that.

Little had she known when she'd woken up this morning with such anticipation, that she would be here, in exile, all her dreams shipwrecked. A noise came from inside the kitchen, and a shadow entered the balcony. Her hopes leapt irrationally—was it Jonathon? She froze, not daring to look around. A click sounded, the shadow was lighting up.

Not Jonathon. Her shoulders slumped. She closed her eyes against it all and allowed Jonathon to materialise, as from tomorrow, she promised herself anew, she would put him out of her mind. She ignored a scoffing sense of déjà vu in favour of another more exciting image unfolding in her mind. Jonathon setting out to find her, say she was on the vineyard, with Jean-Pierre, and they heard a car pull up and it was him. How thrilling would that be? She stopped herself from imagining them running toward each other, arms outstretched. Maybe that was taking it too far. At least she had a shining light inside to warm her as she made her way to bed. And if she could program her dreams, she was going to program Jonathon, in a DJ, with the jacket thrown over his shoulder, white open necked shirt molded to his chest. A smattering of hair peeping out the top, and shirtsleeves folded up to his perfectly formed biceps.

Come on, dreams, do your stuff. Give me a break from this misery.

*

The night air was cold as it buffeted his jacket, but Jonathon couldn't care less. It kept him sharp, and he needed to be alert to figure out what to do. The stars above were lofty, impervious to the pain he was going through. Dammit, he had never let anything stop him from getting what he wanted. And he wanted Pippa. But how was he going to get her?

As the Xplorer dropped him back at the ship, there was a rowdy queue of Marcus's PR team waiting to get on, ably assisted by Fiona. She raised an eyebrow when she spotted him coming off, on his own.

"Well?" She crossed names off the list on her clipboard as the team went onto the boat.

"Well what?" Jonathon grimaced, as if he didn't know what she was talking about.

"Where's Pippa?"

"Hell if I know. She was ashore up until a couple of hours ago, but now, apparently is headed for Queenstown." He blew a long breath out, his gaze absentmindedly following the mist it made.

Fiona nodded slowly, chewing on the end of her pen. "So where would she go from there? Auckland? Could she be heading back to the UK?"

Jonathon looked past her, out into the darkness. "I don't think so. Knowing Pippa, even if only for a short time, I think she would make the most of being on the other side of the world. I don't think she'd go back quite so soon." He folded his arms and tapped one finger against his chin. "But where else would she go?"

"Queenstown is quite an obvious choice." Fiona saw the last remaining passenger onto the boat and gave Phillip and Lee the thumbs up. "Perhaps too obvious."

"Does she know anybody in New Zealand?"

"No. Well, except for Jean-Pierre."

Jonathon's brain snapped to attention. "Jean-Pierre?"

"Yeah." Fiona's eyes gleamed. "And Pippa told me he had offered her a job and everything!"

Hope rose in him like a spring gushing from the ground. *Keep it easy, she may not be there.* Try though he did, it refused to be quashed totally.

"Akoroa. Well, that's where I'm headed as soon as we dock tomorrow."

Fiona smiled at him—a wide, beaming smile. "Okay, let me see what I can do to get you there."

Chapter Sixteen

As she flew over the Southern Alps, Pippa's hopes dipped and refused to soar along with the small Cessna as it caught the wind currents. She had struggled to open her eyes that morning, feeling like she had gone ten emotional rounds during the night.

So much for programming your dreams.

Eddie, Darrel's business associate, was brusque and keen not to chat—which was fortunate, as the noise in the tiny cabin inhibited conversation.

The almost palpable thought of Jonathon hung in the air and her insides turned over as the actuality of life without him slowly became real, stretching out in front of her, dreary and colourless.

The Southern Alps were awesome, but Pippa had to bow her head under the sudden sadness they evoked. She wouldn't have the opportunity to explore them with Jonathon, to go hiking, kayaking, camping in the wild, to be on a snowcapped mountain in the morning, followed by a swim in the sea in the afternoon.

There would be no Jonathon striding out beside her, supporting her when the going got tough, making her laugh when she wanted to cry, and at the end of every day, getting into bed with her. His face wouldn't be the first thing she saw when she woke.

Her sadness yawned wide within her.

It had all been so perfect. Two weeks on board, cooking—something else she loved—then one week off, providing her with the perfect opportunity to explore this largely unspoiled land. And all of it with Jonathon. Did it get any better than that?

Now she had nothing.

No, scratch that. She had a broken heart.

When the plane started circling, Pippa dragged her thoughts back and watched the ground looming, forcing herself to take an interest. So this was where Jean-Pierre had set up his restaurant. They started a slow descent, and soon she could make out the vineyards in sharper detail.

Eddie pointed to a patch of green and shouted, "That's where we're landing." Pippa nodded, hearing the plane's engines throttle down to prepare. It was a hair-raising drop, one that Pippa would normally have loved. But this time, she simply didn't care. So what if they crashed, at least she wouldn't have to battle with the thought that she'd just lost the only man she could ever love.

Walking down the steps, she had to work hard to maintain equanimity but the sight of Jean-Pierre walking toward her invited more tears. As he grew near, he held out his arms to encase her in a hug.

"Alors mon petit chou. N'inquiete pas, tu es ici maintenant. Calme-toi." Folding her in his arms, he murmured French endearments to her. *Don't worry, you're here now. Relax.*

Listening to him, Pippa felt a seismic shift in her tummy, unclogging her emotions and the tears emerged. "Jean-Pierre, I'm such a fool."

"Nonsense. I do not believe it. Come." He gestured toward a waiting car. "You are tired." He kissed the top of her head and turning her to face the car, walked with her.

*

"Mr. Eagleton!" Fiona's voice, high pitched with excitement, leaked through the suite door that had nearly closed behind George Stevenson. They had just finished the contract details, preferring to close the deal now rather than waiting for Queenstown to iron out the last details.

Jonathon pulled the door open wide. "What have you got for me?"

"I've chartered you a plane from Milford Sound. That's your quickest way. And I've booked a taxi in half an hour to pick you up and bring you to the field." She stopped and looked closely at him. "What's wrong?"

He stared at the floor, clenching his jaw. Flying long distance in a jet was just about manageable. Even the *thought* of flying in a small plane, on the other hand, induced nausea.

"You could hire a car and drive, but it would take at least eight hours."

Eight hours? Not an option.

"Nothing's wrong. Thank you."

"Good luck." Fiona smiled with such an assurance that he was going to win Pippa over, and headed off. Jonathon almost believed it himself, but Pippa was a stubborn woman and he sure as hell hadn't a clue how she would react to seeing him again. He could almost taste the sweet relief but he pushed it to one side. She may not want to talk to him.

As he raced through the ship, the certainty that he would find her in Akoroa infused him. This felt so right, unlike yesterday where panic had been a not-too-distant companion. An overwhelming peace calmed him. He would find his girl, and then whatever happened would be purely down to him. If he messed it up, it was his fault, he couldn't blame publicity, ex-boyfriends, misunderstandings about relationships with the boss, anything.

It was all down to him.

After the dithering of the last twenty-four hours, it felt great to have a rock solid purpose. He didn't notice the trip into Milford Sound, purposefully refusing to think about the flight, thinking instead of Pippa and that last betrayed looked as she'd realised Marcus was on board. That look would forever haunt him. He had to convince her of his love.

When he saw the Cessna, he swallowed to get rid of the rush of saliva in his mouth. He was going to fly over the Southern Alps in *that?* His heart thumped, resembling an African drum, hollow and lonely.

He had to do it. It was only three hours out of his life. Everybody flew, he was just being stupid. He couldn't take the chance of driving, she may have left Akorao by then.

This was for Pippa, for love, for the rest of his life.

*

Fred, the pilot, handed him a silver hip flask as he belted up. "Whisky—you look like you'll need it." His expression was wry as he flicked some buttons overhead and the engines roared in response.

Jonathon couldn't reply, only nod in appreciation and take a swallow of the fire water. He handed it back to Fred who waved it away. "It's for you, mate. I don't drink."

With that, the plane was on the move. Jonathon clutched onto his arms of his seat, myriad emotions skidding through him.

Pippa. Think of Pippa. Think of what you're going to say to her.

An image of her, dancing with the Maoris, green eyes sparkling at him and topsy-turvy curls glowing in the firelight changed to her lying beside him in front of the fire, running her hand over his side. Was there a more perfect woman in the world than Pippa Renshaw?

As the plane made its way over the Alps, buffeted by the winds, Jonathon held on to the thought of Pippa loving him and their future life together. His stomach stopped roiling, his head stopped spinning, blood returned to his fingers and toes. What had he been thinking? He didn't have a fear of flying—this was excitement, *adrenaline* twisting through him. His luck was in— the kind of luck that's with someone when they're doing the right thing, finally.

He and Pippa were meant to be.

*

Pippa lay on crisp white cotton sheets under a pretty patchwork quilt and big fluffy pillows in that place between sleeping and waking, relaxed as a rag doll. When she had seen it, her mood had lightened, and despite it being late morning, she'd decided to take a nap. How could she refuse that bed? Jean-Pierre had said his mother had sewn the quilt using an aerial image of the South Island as a pattern.

She swung her feet off the bed to encounter warm flagstones. *I've died and gone to Heaven. If only Jonathon were here.* The thought of him brought a renewed sharp ache to her chest. When would she be free of him? Padding over to the large sash window, her heart softened as the sea spread out before her.

The house that Jean-Pierre shared with Darrel was half an hour from the vineyards. Earlier on, they had come in through the back, and the sound of the waves had lulled her into a deep afternoon sleep—but she hadn't known the house was right there on the beach. Could she go swimming? What the hell, it was just what she needed. The clock said four-thirty, so there was plenty of time before dinner at seven.

She grabbed her swimsuit and a towel and ran down the stairs, calling out for Jean-Pierre. When she didn't get a reply, she scrabbled about in the hall until she found a pencil and phone pad, and hastily wrote a note for him.

The back door of the large kitchen opened onto the beach. She walked down the stony steps, stopping only to take in the long beach as it stretched far from her. The sea was more blue than green, with a light wind whipping up white tipped waves. She could feast her eyes on it for hours. The constant movement and charge of the deep was mesmerizing. It matched her grief. Unchanging, yet constantly in motion, commanding her attention at all times.

She dropped her towel and headed toward the water, her insides already shrinking away from the thought of the cold water.

She waded in quickly, gasping at the cold, then plunged into a wave before swimming as fast as she could.

Her body was soon covered in goose pimples, but it felt so good. As she concentrated on swimming and not freezing to death, it forced all thoughts of Jonathon to the back of her mind. Warming up finally, she flipped over onto her back to float and watch the royal blue sky, with little fluffy clouds scudding over. Seawater kept washing over her face. She flipped into treading water, and it was then that she saw them.

Dolphins.

About ten of them, circling her. She forgot to breathe as she stared in awe. Wow. Dolphins here with her in the wild, letting her share their water, choosing to swim with *her*.

She felt privileged, amazed. Not wanting to make any sudden movements, she kept herself upright, gently treading water. They were so graceful, their curved, shiny, gray bodies breaking out of the water and back in with barely a splash, weaving in and out. She forced rueful tears back as the memory of telling Jonathon about her dream of swimming with dolphins came back to her.

And now look. When she'd least expected it, here they were, bringing her dream alive. But she had shared it with Jonathon, unconsciously adding him. He should be here, with her, swimming with dolphins. Her sadness, a black hole, opened wider to suck all other thoughts in. Leaving her only the thought of him.

With a final circle, the dolphins left her to leap back over the waves into the wild sea. The water cajoled her to lie back and the warm salty tide inveigled the tension from her shoulders, massaging her chest and her limping heart.

Let's face it, she had always known Jonathon was going to be trouble. Her little premonition when she first met him now made perfect sense. And what had she done with her warning? Ignored it, like the fool she was. Instead of protecting herself, she had gone right ahead and fallen in love with her boss. Jonathon Eagleton.

Disaster.

Cold settled into her bones and she struck out for shore, glad of the buoyancy of the seawater. When her hands brushed against the sea bottom, she swung her legs around to kneel.

It was then she saw him.

No way, it couldn't be.

Could it?

Squeezing the excess water from her hair, she tried to focus on the tall figure silhouetted against the sun. There was no way he was here. She stood, feeling the seawater gush down her body, and walked toward him as if pulled by magnets.

*

Jonathon couldn't ever remember being so nervous. He had arrived, bang on the dot of five p.m. The taxi had dropped him at the door of the villa, where knocking had brought no answer. Glad of the reprieve, he'd walked to the beach.

Standing there, gazing unseeingly out to the windy sea, it took a while for him to register the dolphins. His heart puffed like a parachute when he saw Pippa in their midst, a smile on her pretty face. Her green eyes would be shining, her lips looking utterly kissable. He wanted to strip off and go to her.

But no doubt the dolphins would leave with his arrival and Pippa wouldn't be impressed with him. Not the way he wanted their reunion to start. The dolphins bucked and peeled away from her, and Pippa floated. A long, lithe figure.

It was now or never—he had to convince her to love him. When he saw her swim back and stand in the water, he felt like he'd been sucker punched, his breath stolen from him. Water cascaded down her body, highlighting her firm breasts and slim waist in her blue bikini, her hair sexily slicked back. This girl was all-woman and he meant for her to be his.

*

Pippa's consciousness confirmed what she had known all along. It was him.

He bent to pick up her towel, and held it out. Her tongue turned to sandpaper, and her heart pounded erratically in a desperate attempt to maintain her equilibrium. A kaleidoscope of butterflies released deep within her, and her knees wobbled, trying to hold her weight.

One of those butterflies carried a small spark of hope.

She stopped a few feet away from him. She couldn't physically or emotionally go any further. She reached in and pulled her towel from him. Bringing her gaze up, her eyes lit upon his face. His dark eyes were shaded by his frown, and his full bottom lip straightened in a worry line. Stubble shadowed his jaw.

"Pippa." Running both hands agitatedly through his hair, he said more strongly, "Pippa." He held his hand out to her.

She ignored it. Shivering, she wrapped the towel around her shoulders, knowing it couldn't quell the real reason she shivered.

"What are you doing here? Are you looking for Jean-Pierre? He's out on the vineyards. At least I think he is. I know Eddie is here to do some business with him. Over there—"

"I'm here to see you."

"Oh? Well, then I guess it's about the job, so, em, sorry I walked out. I'm cold, do you mind if we carry on this conversation at the house?" She turned to head back.

He reached out his hand and closed it gently on her forearm. "Yes. No."

Hope fizzled. It was only about the job.

"I'll start again. Yes, we can go back to the house but no, why I've come has nothing to do with the job. Well, almost nothing. I do want to apologise for bringing Marcus in." He stopped, and she felt his eyes on her. But try as she did, her gaze refused to budge from the footprints in the sand.

Not trusting herself to speak, she shrugged.

"Juliet had booked Marcus without informing me and we couldn't afford the bad publicity if we cancelled him." He grasped her by one shoulder, his touch drying the remaining drops of seawater and causing her skin to sizzle. He put one hand under her chin and gently brought her head up. His eyes scoured her face, trailing heat. "I'm sorry."

"It's okay." Her voice sounded distant to her, as though it wasn't actually her speaking. But it was the truth, she had gotten over the Gala Dinner. Other, deeper disappointments had taken over. Stepping away from his searing grip, she dropped her chin. "Look, you don't need to worry about me. I'll get another job. Maybe here, maybe London. I don't know yet." She turned to go back to the house.

"No, wait. There's another apology I have to make." His voice so low she could barely hear him.

"There's no need, honestly. Thank you for apologising about last night. Let's just leave it at that." She picked up her flip-flops and began the long hike away from the man she loved.

"Just listen to me, please!" His voice carried an ocean of pleading within it, with a strong undercurrent of deep desire. It brought her to a halt.

"That comment about you and Mulberry. It was ridiculous, and I knew deep down that you never would have done something like that. I *knew*, yet still I said it to you. And why? Because I wanted to sabotage what was growing so passionately between us. I was afraid—of my reputation, of being compared to *him*, of you being the butt end of jokes, but most of all..." He walked around to stand in front of her, his face ravaged by storms. "I was afraid of loving you. And you know what?" He gave a bitter laugh. "That fear is nothing compared to what I feel now." He grabbed her hand and it was as though he grabbed her heart, stopping all oxygen to her brain. She was going lightheaded. "I'm afraid to the bones of never seeing you again. Of being deprived of your smile, your caress, your quirky way of looking at things. Look at me, dammit!"

*

He had lost her. She couldn't even bear to look at him. As he watched and waited, her frown dissolved and her eyes opened. She looked out to sea and drew a deep breath.

"I'm sorry too. About that day, you know." She finally looked at him, softness removing the hard edges that had temporarily shown in her face. "I freaked out because I had woken up after a wonderful night with you to find myself alone. I knew something was wrong. Instead of finding out it was because you were in love with Juliet, or that you regretted what had happened, I attacked you and walked off. It was easier to cope that way, rather than finding out the truth. A truth I was sure I couldn't bear."

Jonathon reached out and pulled her unresistingly into his arms. She stood quiescent but he could feel her heart beating as erratically as his.

Okay this was it. This was the moment.

"One more thing." He felt her nod. "When I said I could fall in love with you, I wasn't being honest." He felt her pulling back from him, but he sure as hell wasn't letting go. "Wait a minute, woman! I wasn't being honest because, because...I *am* in love with you." He stopped and leaned back so he could see her beloved face, her wide turquoise eyes sparkling like the sun over water, cute freckles dotted over her nose, and that sweet, kissable, oft dreamed about, rosebud mouth. "Always have been, always will be. The moment you tumbled into that hotel's reception, I started falling in love with you. I know it's *crazy*..." He shouted the word at the sky. "We've only known each other for eleven short days, but I just know that you and I, we're right together."

She blinked at him, a long, lazy closing of her eyes that only enhanced her irises, making her all eyes as she gazed into him.

"Speak! Say something." He let go of her abruptly. "I'm just a fool, aren't I?"

She didn't feel the same way. His heart plummeted as though he himself had just dived straight into the cold sea water.

Pippa's slender fingers reached for his, and pulling his hand to her mouth, she dropped a kiss in his palm, then curled his fingers over it.

"Right there. You have me right there, in the palm of your hand." She brought her soft hands up to his face and cupped it, eyes luminous with unshed tears. "I'm in love with you too."

His heart leapt, a shooting star, trailing gladness around his body, out to his fingertips that were turning white as he held his hand closed tight over her kiss. Pippa glowed as she looked at him and he gazed back, drinking in his fill of her. Eyes fastening on her mouth, he lowered his head and her lips met his shyly. He deepened the kiss, lips moving restlessly on hers, and pressed her body hard against his.

"I love you, Pippa," he whispered against her kiss. "Be mine."

*

Pippa heard his words through an intoxicated haze. He loved her, he did! Her lips curved, and she felt love coursing through her, leaving no cell unturned.

Then a thought struck her and she struggled out of his arms. "But what about you being CEO and all that stuff? Or were you thinking since I walked out, I don't work for you anymore?"

Jonathon sighed good-naturedly. He picked up a curl and wound his finger through it.

"You're a fantastic chef, Pippa, I don't want to lose you as head chef. All your staff were singing your praises, and you were sorely missed last night. I'm going to be based in Auckland and Sydney for the time being, but I don't plan on working for Queen Cruises longer than two years anyway. Besides..." He looked out of the corner of his eyes at her, a mischievous glint to them.

"Besides?" What was he thinking?

"If we got married, then that should solve that little problem."

"Married?" Pippa spluttered the word. He couldn't mean it.

"Pippa, look, I love you. Yes, it's mad, but heck, who cares? We were made for each other. Let's get married and spend the rest of our lives getting to know each other. And, if you want, we can have a dozen kids and roam this crazy countryside together. What do you say?"

She couldn't say anything. Happiness bubbled up from her core, a volcano erupting with the sheer headiness of the man she loved proposing to her. When did life get so good? The sun shone down with renewed heat, and the sand she stood on sparkled into life. She gazed up into his adored face and ran a finger down the side of it, enjoying the feeling of the hard edge of his jaw, the raspy stubble.

"What do I say? I say yes!" She was drunk on love. A thrill ran through her intoxication, a little red hot devil surfing the emotion.

He wrapped her in his arms, pulling her head into the crook of his neck. How had she, Pippa Renshaw, gotten so lucky?

"I have to tell you, Ms. Renshaw, you have made me the happiest man in the whole..." he kissed her on the forehead, "wide..." the tip of her nose, "wonderful..." and he dropped his warm full lips on hers in a hard kiss that promised more soon, "world today. I am going to discover the things that make you smile your sunny smile and laugh in that sexy way of yours. Once I know all your hot buttons, I will make sure that each and every one of them is pressed every day."

The look of tenderness on his face was the purest expression Pippa had ever seen, and it unfurled a flower deep within her, sending contentment and delightedness in each direction until her body was a mass of happiness.

He pulled away from her only to sweep one arm under her legs to lift her up against his hard, masculine chest. A low growl turned the happiness to heat—molten lava that lapped at her core, sending shivers of anticipation rocketing through her.

"Wait!" Pippa's voice squeaked, her throat unnaturally tight. "My towel fell off!"

"Woman," Jonathon said as he glanced down at her, the tender look turning dark with desire. He didn't break stride. "You won't need that where we're going."

About the Author

Cait O'Sullivan is a romance author with a love of words and magic, having had the good fortune to grow up in Ireland. The wanderlust in her blood sent her out to travel the world and now, residing in a leafy suburb of London, it is her thoughts and memories that journey far and wide in order to create her stories.

Learn more about her at:
www.caitosullivan.blogspot.com

To see her updates, come to:
www.facebook.com/CaitOSullivanAuthor
https://twitter.com/romanticait

In the mood for more Crimson Romance? Check out *California Wine* by Casey Dawes at *CrimsonRomance.com*.